Thug Holiday Thanksgiving Edition

Written by:

Patrice Balark

Dani Littlepage

J. Dominique

Twyla T.

Copyright:

Publisher's Note:

Published by Cole Hart Signature

Dedication:

This book is dedicated to the dopest publisher in the game, Cole Hart!

Salute!!!

Chapter 1

Alexis sat on the burgundy couch with her arms folded across her chest, while she listened to Marcus give her yet another lecture. She had an Advanced Accounting class in an hour that consisted of Professor Collins running his mouth for two hours straight, so the last thing she needed now was a sermon from one of her best friends.

"Bitch, you can sit there and roll your eyes all you want to, but you know I'm right," Marcus said placing his hands on his chubby hips.

"Bitch, please! Number one, I'm grown, I can do what the fuck I wanna do and number two, you just hating," Alexis replied, standing to her feet.

"Haaattttiiinnnnggggg on what, darling? Look at me, what reason do I have to hate?" Marcus boasted as he did a full spin, flipping his imaginary weave off his shoulders.

Alexis couldn't help but laugh at her best friend of three years. Not only was Marcus dramatic, he was a clown that belonged with Barnum and Bailey.

"Look friend, I get what you saying, but I know what I'm doing; I got this," Lexi reminded him while she grabbed a bottle of Ice Mountain water from the refrigerator.

"Ok, because I'll hate for some shit to happen to you. You playing with fire and these niggaz don't play about two things; their feelings and their grandma. And bitttccchhhhhh, I ain't got time to be fighting because these lil hoodlums you deal with, honey, they only know about nine millimeters and AKs," Marcus joked.

Lexi bent over in laughter. Marcus was one of the funniest people she ever met. They became friend's freshman year at Clark University in Atlanta. From the beginning, they had so much in common. Both of them were southern raised; Lexi reigned in from Jackson, Mississippi, while Marcus was a Bama boy. After they both realized they were Accounting majors, they adjusted their schedules and classes and had been joined at the hip ever since.

"Aye, I'm about to FaceTime him right now, be quiet," Lexi warned Marcus while she grabbed her iPhone 7 Plus off the glass coffee table in the middle of Marcus's one bedroom apartment.

Lexi looked at herself in the phone and fixed her long jet-black curly weave while she waited on J.R. to answer. Just as she was about to end the call, he picked up.

"What up, shordy?" he said with a blunt in his hand.

"What's up? What you doing?" she quizzed.

"Shit, about to make a run with the guys, what you on?" he shot back.

"Nothing, about to head to class. I was hoping I could see you before I went though," she said in a flirty tone that usually worked like a charm.

"Shiddddd.... My bad shordy, I got some business to take care of right now. Imma hit yo line and fuck around and slide through later.... Aight?" J.R. replied, not even looking at the phone.

"YUP!" was all Lexi said before she ended the call.

J.R. was one of Lexi's latest victims. She ran into him about a month ago while at the Waffle House with

Marcus and her other best friend, Bre. J.R. wasn't like the other Atlanta niggaz she was used to meeting; he had that East Coast swag, considering the fact he was originally from Philly. He stood about 6'3 with a skinny nigga frame, just the way she liked it. Instead of a mouth full of gold like the rest of them country fools, he had a set of pearly whites accompanied by one dimple on the right side of his face. He had a fair medium brown complexion, with a fresh tapper and lining; however, he wore his hair a few inches shy of a fro, with the nappy look that the guys seemed to be into now of days. What seemed to turn her on the most though, was the way the Gucci jogging suit hung off his body and those all wheat loose-laced Timbs on his feet. J.R. had on just the right amount of jewelry, not so much to be flashy, but just enough to show niggaz he wasn't a broke nigga. When he approached her, Lexi thought of him as nothing but another nigga who could be her sponsor; however, she was in for a rude awakening.

"Damn, did he just play Sexy Lexi like that?" Marcus laughed, while sticking his tongue out at Alexis.

"Fuck you!" she replied, sticking up her middle finger and snatching her car keys off of that same glass table.

"I'm out of here.... bitch, walk to class!" she continued, chucking up the deuces at Marcus and walking out the door.

By the time she made it to the elevator, he was behind her with his book bag in hand.

"Girl, you so sensitive, you know I be just playing," he said, buttering her up and out of breath from the short jog down the hall.

"Sensitive my ass, and yo ass just need a ride; get in," she said, rolling her eyes and hitting the alarm on her 2016 Midnight blue Mercedes Benz.

They rode the short ride to campus in silence. Not only did Lexi not want to go to class, she also dreaded going to work afterwards because she was going to be tired as fuck. She thought about quitting time after time, but she knew the lifestyle she was accustomed to wouldn't allow that, so she pushed that idea to the back of her head and headed into class.

Professor Collins must have been in a good mood this Friday evening because he dismissed class early, but not before reminding everybody of the twenty-page paper that was due after Thanksgiving break, which was two weeks away. Lexi was good with time management because she was half way done with the assignment already and planned on completing it ahead of time. She had a date with Jay Z at his sold out "4:44" tour in New York for Thanksgiving break.

"So, are you going back to the apartment complex or are you heading straight to work?" Marcus asked while they walked to the car.

"I'm going straight in, it's almost eight. I can chill for a minute and grab something to eat before I start. You finna ride with me?" she asked.

"Yeah, my bae not answering the phone, so I guess I can tag along," Marcus agreed.

Regardless of the time of day, Atlanta traffic was a bitch; what should have only been a thirty-minute drive, turned into an hour. Lexi figured that some type of concert must have been going on tonight because the streets of ATL was lit.

Once Lexi finally arrived, she found a park not too far from the door, rolled her windows down, and grabbed the blunt she rolled up back at Marcus's house from her Chanel bag and lit it. She inhaled the smoke and closed her eyes, filling her lungs with the strong weed before exhaling through her nose.

"Aye, you ever think about staying here after graduation?" Lexi asked Marcus while she passed him the blunt.

"All the time; I don't think I could go back to Alabama after being exposed to this," he stated.

"Yeah, me either. I been trying to think of ways to tell my parents without feeling bad."

"Feeling bad… feeling bad for what?" Marcus questioned.

"I mean, it's like, everybody go to college and dip out on them. Two of my older sisters, Alyssa and Anastasia, live in New York. Andrea is the only one still in Mississippi," she explained.

"Bitch, please do what makes Alexis happy. Fuck all that other shit," Marcus snapped.

Just as Lexi was about to respond to him, her phone rang. "Speaking of the devil, this Andrea right here," Lexi stated, holding up her index finger motioning for Marcus to give her a minute.

Lexi talked to her older sister for a cool three minutes before she ended the call.

"See, that's the shit I be talking about," Lexi groaned, snatching the blunt from Marcus and hitting it hard.

"Hold up now, what happened?" a puzzled Marcus asked.

"That was Drea, she wants all of us to come home for Thanksgiving. Even after I told the bitch I had plans, she dismissed what I said by saying she'll reimburse me for my concert tickets and she's expecting me to be there."

"So, what you gon do?" Marcus asked.

"I don't know man, but that shit just blew my night."

"Well, that's yo fault. You let them take advantage of you because you are the baby…."

"It's just that they expect so much out of me. My father is a Pastor of his own church and my mom is a retired school principal. All three of my sisters has finished college; Alyssa got a Bachelor's in Criminal Justice, Anastasia has her own business, and Andrea is a lawyer…… I'm supposed to finish this raggedy ass Bachelor's Degree in accounting and make six figures, too."

"Well, what will make Alexis happy?" Marcus asked.

"That's the crazy part, I don't know. I'm only twenty, I don't have life figured out yet, but what I do know is, I probably make more money a year than any of my sisters." Lexi bragged.

"Shid, I've seen you on that pole, so I'm pretty sure you do, too. I'd just hate to be there when your perfect little family finds out that the baby girl of the Holiday sisters is Blue Flames top dancer," Marcus stated.

"Yeah, that's the thing, they could never find out. But, in the meantime, I'm about to take all these thirsty niggaz rent money; let's go!" Lexi said, putting out the blunt and heading into the club that changed her life two years ago.

Chapter 2

Alyssa sat in her car a moment longer, after she received a call from her oldest sister, Andrea, about returning home for the Thanksgiving holiday. She wasn't thrilled about the idea, but she would have to think about that at another time. Alyssa had more important things to attend to. She put her phone on mute before she tossed it in her purse and got out of her car. She wasn't thrilled about coming in for a last-minute meeting in the evening time on a supposed to be off day, but she had to do what she had to do to make a name for herself. Besides, it was only her second week of "real" work, and she couldn't deny that she was excited as hell. Alyssa clicked the button to lock her car doors as she made her way inside the federal building.

Alyssa flashed her badge in front of the sensor upon entering the building, walked towards the elevator, and rode it to the fourth floor. When she arrived at her floor, she stepped off, walked through the double glass doors, and headed straight to her desk. When she was seated, she felt her phone vibrating in her purse. Alyssa pulled out her phone and cussed when she saw it was her sister, Anastasia, calling. She placed her phone face down on her desk and began to work.

Alyssa was the third of four sisters and had a Bachelor's degree in Criminal Justice, but when she didn't land the job she wanted, she secretly furthered her career. To help her sister out, and also earn a little pocket change, Alyssa began working at Anastasia's boutique. Alyssa enjoyed working with at the boutique with her sister and started out as the stellar employee, but for the past few months, working at the boutique had come second to training to become an FBI agent. When she wasn't showing up late for work, she didn't show up at all. Anastasia and Alyssa were the closet and she wanted to let her sister know about her new career, but she figured that it was best to keep it to herself.

"Alyssa, we're gathering in the conference room," her co-worker tapped on the door and leaned her head in to say. That instantly brought her back to reality.

"Okay. Here I come," Alyssa responded.

She got up from her desk and followed her co-worker into the conference room, where three other people were already seated at the table. When they were seated, the head of their department began to brief them on the subject at hand. He placed a picture on the table of a young man by the name of D'Mani Mitchell, who was a well-known and respected drug lord. He gave them the basics about the subject at hand like where he lived, who he communicated with, and how long he was in the game, but that's all the information he could give them. Their mission was to gather solid evidence, so that they could make an arrest and with that being said, they were dismissed.

Alyssa went back to her desk to finish up some paperwork before she left for the day. As soon as she was safe in her car, she pulled out her phone and attached her earphones to it before she called her sister. She placed the key in the ignition, brought the car to life, and pulled out of the parking lot when her sister answered the phone.

"Bitch, where the fuck are you? You were supposed to be here at nine this morning?" Anastasia yelled.

"I'm sorry, Stasia, but I had something else to take care of."

"You always got something to take care of that you have yet to tell me about," Anastasia fumed.

"We've been through this already. Anyway, what did you call me for?" Alyssa sighed.

"To see if Andrea called you and to tell you that you're fired."

"Yeah, she called and as far as being fired, I appreciate it." Alyssa chuckled.

Before her sister could respond, Alyssa's phone beeped, indicating that she had a call waiting. She glanced at her phone and saw that it was her boyfriend calling. She quickly ended the call with her sister and answered her other line.

"Hey Bae. What's going on?"

"Nothing much. Just got to the television station so we can start taping the show," Corey answered. "What you got going on?"

"Nothing. About to head home and chill for a minute. Why?"

"I wanted to know if you were available for dinner tonight. There is something I need to talk to you about?"

"Yeah, I'm available." She smiled. "What do we need to talk about?" Alyssa inquired.

"I'll tell you when I see you tonight. Be ready by 7:30 p.m. I love you!" Corey told her.

"I love you, too!" Alyssa exclaimed.

She drove the rest of the way home with her head full of thoughts as to what her man wanted to talk to her about. They had been dating for over a year, but known each other since their freshman year of college. Corey was the starting point guard of their school's basketball team and was sure to be the next big NBA sensation, but when he tore his ACL his junior year, that ended his basketball career. When he graduated, he got a job as a sports commentator. It was the only way to keep him close to the game he loved.

When she pulled up to her condo in downtown New York, Alyssa parked her car, locked the doors, and made her way inside. Alyssa placed her keys on the hook and dragged herself to her room where she flopped down on her bed and stared at the ceiling as an uneasy feeling began to settle in her stomach about going home to Mississippi for the holidays.

Chapter 3

"Ahh fuck, Ana! I'm bouta cum!" *Good, then maybe I can get some sleep*, Anastasia thought to herself as her husband of six years gyrated on top of her. Honest to God, the whole thing had her feeling like Whitney Houston in *Waiting to Exhale*, when she was fucking the dude that growled. Anastasia figured she'd help him out and get him the fuck off of her, so she used one of her perfected fake orgasms knowing it would push him over the edge.

"Mmm mmh, Rich; that feels so good! You got this pussy creamin!" she moaned loudly hoping that she didn't wake up their five-year-old son, Kyler.

Anastasia really hadn't meant to be so loud, but she didn't think she could handle another minute of being laid up under his ass. Their sex sessions were already few and far between, and only lasted about ten minutes at best. Between the sweating, weak ass thrusts, and less than average dick, Anastasia didn't know what was worse. Most times, she didn't mind letting him get his off while she planned her day or thought over different designs for her small boutique, but today wasn't one of those times.

Things had not been going her way that day; starting with her older sister, Andrea, calling about coming home for the holidays first thing in the morning. The last thing she was thinking about was going back to hick ass Mississippi for Thanksgiving. Anastasia already knew that the only thing she'd be going home to was fighting with Andrea's goody two shoe ass, being extremely prim and proper for her parents, whatever antics their baby sister, Alexis, had going on, and fattening food. She hadn't been home in the last three years and she didn't feel like she should go back for another three. On top of that, her other sister, Alyssa, that worked in her boutique had been missing shifts and today had been no different. Honestly, Anastasia was a little bothered by the fact that she didn't know what was going on with her. Out of all of the sisters, her and Alyssa were the closest; thus, the reason they both lived in New York. After she graduated, got a job, and quit for no apparent reason other than saying she didn't like it, Anastasia had given her the job until she figured out her next move, but for the last month or so she had been coming in late or missing days. Usually they would talk about any and everything, but lately she'd been really distant and sneaky even. Her doing a no call no show today had put Anastasia in a tight spot because she had to come in and work with the new trainee, which put a stop to her plans of meeting up with her boo. The thought of him alone forced an orgasm where there hadn't been one before, because Rich for damn sure didn't give it to her.

"Fuck yesssss!" she involuntarily cried out, barely stopping herself from calling out her bae's name. With her eyes closed, she rode the waves of her dull orgasm until Richard opened his mouth and ruined the moment forcing them right back open.

"See, daddy still got it." He cheesed down at her through his glasses and she fought not to frown up at him. Mustering up a smile to match the goofy one he wore, she looked right up at him and lied.

"Hell, yeah you do honey." Placing a light peck on her lips like only his corny ass could, he slipped his now limp dick out of her and rolled over onto his side of their California king bed. Not wanting to have to talk to him at all she turned her back to him, but that didn't stop him from sliding closer and putting his arms around her.

"If that didn't put a baby in there, then I don't know what will," Richard said into her ear making her body go rigid.

"Mmh hmm," was all she could manage to get out.

The last thing Anastasia wanted was another baby by him. She'd gone so far as to get put on the depo shot to ensure that she wouldn't get pregnant while he spent his time trying to nut in her. He'd gotten lucky with Kyler due to a malfunction while she was on the pill, but that wouldn't be happening again. She loved Kyler to death and honestly couldn't imagine her life without him, but he was just something else that tied her to her husband. It was bad enough that Anastasia already felt stuck, trapped even in this marriage; another baby would only make her feel worse. Not that she had any intentions on leaving Richard, but she wanted to keep the option open.

She thought back to how her father had basically shoved him down her throat as soon as she graduated. It was like he wanted to make sure at least one of his daughters got married and so far, only Anastasia had a husband, so he must have known something she didn't know. The pressure to please their parents had always forced the girls into situations they didn't want to be in… case in point, Anastasia and her lame ass husband. That was one of the very reasons that she couldn't leave him for the man she really loved.

From the moment, she'd met him she knew his ass was a thug. That nigga embodied the streets, he was a walking, talking, real life book bae and she just had to have him the minute he stepped foot inside of her store. Their meeting still gave her chills.

She was alone in the store because Alyssa had called off with her flaky ass. Her head was down looking over the latest credit card bill from one of her many shopping trips. It was extremely high, but she knew Richard wasn't going to say shit since he hadn't been spending much time at home lately. The bell from the door caused her to look up with her sales lady smile, until her eyes landed on the most delicious looking piece of chocolate that she'd ever seen. Instantly, her mouth dropped open and she had to stop herself from drooling. He had to be at least 6'2" with a fresh Caesar cut and one of those panty soaking thick beards. His ass knew he looked damn good, too, because once his eyes met hers he licked his thick lips, then smirked like he knew what I was thinking, giving me a glimpse of his gold fronts. Anastasia took in his appearance. Knowing that even though he was dressed down in some black Jordan sweatpants and a black V-neck, with long Jordan socks and Gucci slides, he was still sexy in her eyes. Stuck in place, Anastasia waited until he approached the counter where she sat, scared that if she stood up he would notice the wet spot that she was sure showed through her gray leggings.

"Can I get some assistance?" he asked, stopping in front of her. It took a moment for her to get her shit together enough to answer him with actual words.

"Uh...yes. How may I help you?"

Would you believe that nigga actually smiled and said, "Well, first you can let me help you take care of that orgasm you need, so you can do your job."

"Excuse me," she asked, thinking that she couldn't have heard him right. Was it that obvious that she was in dire need of a good nut?

"You heard me," he told her, stepping around the counter. Still sitting, Anastasia was eye level with his waist and she couldn't help but to take in the view of his dick print. Even in black sweat pants she could see it and she wondered briefly if he was wearing draws. When Anastasia realized what she was considering and where she was, she stood up and put both of her hands up to stop him from coming closer.

"First of all, I'm married and even if I wasn't, what you just suggested was extremely inappropriate." She tried to keep her voice from coming out shaky and stop her heart from beating through her chest. Truth was, she was definitely in need of an orgasm and she was willing to bet he could do the job.

"Can't be too inappropriate...yo nipples bouta bust outta that shirt, and I know that pussy leakin." He bit into his bottom lip. "Let me do what yo husband can't."

Anastasia just knew she should have been offended by this nigga. Everything that had come out of his mouth after "can I get some assistance," had been rude and forward as hell, but she couldn't deny the ache between her legs while he stood before her. Without warning, he came into her personal space, enveloping her in his arms and she fit right into them. Those sexy ass lips were on hers before she could even think to get away. While his tongue explored her mouth, all she could think about was how good it felt for a nigga to take it. For the first time, her mind was not on her husband or her son.

The fact that she couldn't stop herself, both scared and excited her at the same time and she didn't object when his hands began to explore her body. A moan escaped her lips and she wrapped both arms around his neck, pulling him closer.

"So, you tryna get this dick or nah?" he asked, breaking their kiss and looking into her eyes. Everything in her body was telling her to say yes and that's exactly what she did. She nodded, too ashamed to speak, but not enough to deny him.He grinned wide before easing her leggings down and sitting her on top of the counter, so that he could take them completely off.

"First, I'm bouta suck the soul out yo pussy, till you can't feel yo legs," he told her as he kissed up the inside of her smooth caramel thighs. "Then, I'ma fuck you till yo body give out."

Anastasia shuddered at the thought of him being able to do any of what he was saying. She was so wet that her ass was sticking to the counter she sat on and he hadn't even touched her yet. Richard acted like he was scared to taste her. When he did attempt to do it, it was so horrible that she always ended up stopping him, but she could already tell that this nigga whose name she didn't even know yet, was a cookie monster for real. The way he was looking at her center alone let her know that she was in for a damn good nut and she needed it. With his eyes on her, he wrapped his lips around her clit and sucked gently.

"Mmh shit," she cried as his tongue assaulted her most sensitive area with precision.

He alternated between nibbling and flicking his tongue across her nub before dipping it inside of her. Every time she tried to scoot away because the pressure was too much, he'd tighten the hold that he had on her thighs and pull her back to him. She didn't know how many times she came after that; she lost track at two and just when she didn't think she could take anymore, he lapped at her center, then stuck a finger in her ass, instantly sending her spiraling out of control. Anastasia no longer had control of her limbs at that point and couldn't imagine being able to have another orgasm after that, but the mystery thug wasn't done. Standing tall, he wiped his mouth and pulled down his sweats letting loose the python he called a dick. It was so pretty and thick, Anastasia wanted to put it in her mouth to see if it tasted as chocolatey as it looked.

"Nah nah nah, it's all about you this go round," he said in a husky voice as he pulled a condom from his pocket and slipped it on, throwing the wrapper on the floor. Anastasia began to lie back, but he stopped her again.

"Nah ma, get up and bend yo ass over."

If her legs would have permitted, she would have hopped right down off the counter, but them bitches were numb, so he had to help her down. He turned her body away from him and laid her down flat on her stomach, with a hand on the back of her head. She whimpered softly as he teased her with the tip, first circling her clit, then her hole before plunging into her.

"Ooh fuck!" she stretched her arms trying to grab ahold of the counter to steady herself as he stroked her body first fast, then slow. The nigga was so deep she could feel it in her chest, but she wouldn't dare stop him because this was the most painful pleasure she'd ever experienced.

"You love this dick, huh?" he teased, wrapping a hand around her low ponytail and yanking her head back. Unsure of really what to say, Anastasia remained quiet only releasing a moan.

"Oh, you want a nigga to stop huh?"

"No!" Her eyes snapped open when he pulled himself out to the tip.

"Then, tell daddy what he wanna hear. You love this thug dick, right?" he coaxed, slipping back inside of her and stroking real slow and long.

"Mmm damn! Yesssss, I looovve ittttt!" she hissed feeling herself building for another release.

"Fuck this pussy tight." He damn near whispered, leaning over and fondling her sore clit.

"Oh my God... oh, my God!" she placed her hand on top of his pressing it harder against herself until she exploded all over him, but he didn't stop until he gave her another orgasm before finally filling up the condom himself.

Finally, worn out, he laid down on her back. The both of them trying to catch their breaths, and just like that, Anastasia had gotten some real dick in her life. After laughing about the situation together they exchanged numbers so that they could keep in touch; even though Anastasia had no intentions on seeing him again. Somehow though, she'd ended up calling on one of those nights when Richard had left her unsatisfied and they'd been rocking ever since.

Anastasia never would have thought that she would fall in love with a man like him, but she couldn't see herself living without him at this point. Then again, she couldn't see herself living without Richard, but him and D'mani were two different types of men. She had tried fighting off the love she had for him in order to fulfill her sense of obligation to Richard, but more and more she was beginning to lean closer to D'mani and picture a life with him. There was no denying she loved her some D'mani Mitchell. He was all she could think about as she drifted off to sleep…

Chapter 4

"Your honor, my client has receipts of everything that he has bought for his child, videos of time spent together, as well as documentation of calls and text messages where the mother has threatened his rights if he doesn't adhere to her sexual demands," Andrea Holiday argued.

"He lying and she lying for him. I don't want that lil dick fucker!" the girl cut Andrea off and yelled from the other side of the courtroom.

Andrea saw that her client was about to retaliate, but she put her hand up and silenced him instantly. The baby mother had reacted just how she wanted her to, and the case was headed in the right direction. She had been down the current road several times before in her five-year career as a family law attorney. Andrea looked over at William Benson, a well-known lawyer in the Golden Triangle Area who sat on a high horse and felt like he couldn't be beaten. His face was red as a stop sign as he tried to calm his client down. Andrea had never gone up against him, but she was never intimidated by him or his status and it showed on her mocha colored skin tone and posture. Andrea stood five feet five in a black and white pin striped pencil skirt that showed off her wide hips and the matching blazer complimented by a pair of six-inch Jessica Simpson pumps with her confidence level through the roof.

"Attorney Benson, you're going to have to control your client or she will be held in contempt of court," Judge Loper said after he banged his gavel a couple of times.

"Your honor, may we have a short recess?" Attorney Benson requested.

"Be back in fifteen minutes," Judge Loper stated and banged his gavel with irritation etched in his voice.

"I'll be back in twelve minutes sharp, you do the same," Andrea told her client after she closed her briefcase, then exited the courtroom.

Benson was known for requesting recesses when things didn't go in his favor. It was clear by the way that he walked into court that he felt like he had the case in the bag. Andrea, on the other hand, took nothing for granted, which was why she did her homework. The case was pretty much over, but Andrea wasn't going to fuss about the break because she could use the time to make a phone call or two to her sisters. She had spoken with Anastasia first thing that morning and the conversation didn't go too well, but Andrea threatened her ass to get home for the holidays. There was sure to be tension, but it would be worth it because the girls needed to come and see their parents. She placed a call to her baby sister, Alexis. Andrea knew that it was a good chance that Lexi was in class, but she called anyway. As the phone rang, thoughts of the relationships she had with her sisters ran through her mind, and it couldn't be denied that she was the closest to the baby of the bunch, Alexis.

"Heeyyy sis!" Lexi sang when she answered after the third ring.

"Hey Lex… what are you doing?" Drea quizzed.

"I'll have you know that I'm headed to class… you should be so proud of me," Lexi beamed.

"I am proud of you lil sis… I'll be even more proud when I see you in two weeks for Thanksgiving," Drea stated.

"Noooo, I'm goin to New York to see Shawn Corey Carter, bitch!" Lexi whined.

"Who?" Drea queried.

"Ugghhh… Jay Z, Drea," Lexi clarified.

"You're coming home for Thanksgiving… not that I should, but I'll refund you for those tickets because I'm surprising mommy and daddy by getting everyone together. See you in two weeks… love you, bye," Drea confirmed and hung up before Lexi could protest any further.

Instead of calling Alyssa, Andrea decided to go to the restroom before court was back in session. As she made her way down the hall, her phone vibrated and she rolled her eyes when she saw the name that she had saved as 'Jackass' on the screen of her iPhone 8 plus. Andrea had gone out on a date with the guy a couple of weeks ago. She thought that she had finally found someone with potential, until the check came and he dismissed himself and went to the bathroom only to never return. Andrea sent the call to voicemail and made her way on inside the bathroom to relieve her bladder. Love and relationships was something that she didn't even want to think about.

When Andrea was done, she washed her hands, dried them off, then made her way back into the courtroom. She saw that her client was already in his seat and briefly wondered if he had even gotten up after she left. Andrea was very firm about promptness and made it aware to all of her clients upfront. After taking her seat and making small talk with her client, court was back in session within five minutes. Andrea smiled about forty-five minutes later and shook her clients hand after he was awarded custody if his five-year-old son. They agreed that if the mother completed a rehab program, she could have visitation rights. It wasn't normal for a judge to take a child away from the mother, but after Andrea dug up information and found out what they were up against, Ray Charles could see that the child would have a more stable environment with his hard-working father.

"Thank you so much, Ms. Holiday. I can't thank you enough," her client told her after court was adjourned.

"Thank you for giving me the opportunity. Now, you go and get your son," Andrea said and patted him on the back.

Andrea walked outside and the temperature had dropped tremendously. She almost thought that winter was going to skip Mississippi, but it seemed like it was about to rear its ugly head soon. Drea hit the button on her keyless entry pad and unlocked her 2017 black S450 4Matic Mercedes Benz. It was a gift that she bought herself for her birthday at the beginning of the year and she loved it. Andrea thought about grabbing some lunch since she was off for the day, but she knew that her mom would have something prepared, so she left downtown Jackson and headed towards Madison where her parents resided, and where she lived right next door in the guest house. On the way, she called the last of the sisters, Alyssa and said a silent prayer that she would answer, so that she could have everyone squared away. Andrea sighed and dialed the number for her secretive ass sister.

"These lil hoes gotta come home, so I can find out what's really goin on with them," Andrea fussed under her breath as she waited on Alyssa to answer.

Chapter 5

"Said little bitch, you can't fuck with me

If you wanted to

These expensive, these is red bottoms

These is bloody shoes…"

Alexis danced in the full-length mirror that hung on the wall of the three-bedroom apartment she shared with her best friend, Bre, as she listened to music. Cardi B. had become one of Alexis's favorite artist, she even referred to her as her long-lost sister because her and the rapper had so much in common. Outside of stripping, many people told her that she resembled the Dominican feisty reality star. Alexis stood about 5'5, small in stature, but thicker than your favorite Instagram model. She had hips and ass that made everyone think she was fresh off of Dr. Miami's surgeon's table, but truth be told, she got it from her momma. Alexis, along with all three of her sisters was thick in all the right places, but it seemed as if Lexi was the only one to use what she got to get what she wanted. Alexis wore her jet black twenty-eight inches of Mink Brazilian hair down her back. Her soft light mocha complexion was blemish and pimple free.

It was a little after 7 a.m. on Saturday morning, and she had just counted all the proceeds that she made the night before from dancing. It was two weekends from Thanksgiving, but her eyes lit up like a Christmas tree when she realized she racked in five grand. Friday nights at Blue Flame was crazy like that, outside from working the pole twice, she had a few private sessions, in which her clients were very generous. Lexi's pussy creamed at the thought of all the money she made last night and she damn near came just thinking about how she could double her profits later that night.

Stripping wasn't something that she was proud of, but she was accustomed to having the finer things in life. Growing up the youngest, her parents wasn't rich, but Lexi got whatever her heart desired, whether it was the hottest fashion, the latest Mikes, or even the fact that she had a brand-new car the day she got her driver license. She was blessed and planned on maintaining that lifestyle, even if that meant selling her soul to the devil himself. Lexi grabbed her vibrating cell phone, disconnected it from the Bluetooth speaker in her room and answered by the second ring.

"Heyyyy mommmmyyy!!!" she sang into the phone.

"Hey baby, what you doing?" Mrs. Holiday asked in her usual chipper voice.

Lexi and her mom spoke every single morning around the same time. It was a ritual they started when she went away to school. Out of everybody in her family, Lexi was the closest to her mom, then her oldest sister, Drea. She loved her father and other siblings dearly, she just bonded with them more so than the others.

"I'm not doing anything mom. Just woke up, about to make me something to eat, then go shopping," Lexi replied.

"Yes, you need to eat something. I swear I know you only been eating junk food since you been away, that's why I want you home for Thanksgiving, so you can get a good home cooked meal baby. How's school?" Mrs. Holiday rambled on.

"I take my midterm before the holiday and I know I'm going to ace that. I'm glad this is my last year, I'm so tired of school," Lexi admitted honestly.

"Well baby, you better get untired, you still have to get through grad school. Have you decided where you going yet?" her mom asked.

Alexis rolled her eyes to the back of her head. Although she loved her mom, she was getting on her fucking nerves, steady forcing grad school on her. Truth be told, Lexi barely went to college in the first place. Her parents would have had a heart attack had she not, so she went because she felt she at least owed them that much. She was so unsure about what she wanted to do with her life at this point and seeing all the money she was making dancing, she dreaded a real nine to five career even more now.

"Well mom, I don't know yet, I still have time to think about it," Lexi finally responded.

"Time? Baby, this year is almost over with, graduation is in June and I went online, the deadline for submitting your application is approaching as well. I knew you was going to slow drag, so I took the liberty and emailed you some grad schools back here in Mississippi. Think about how much money we will all save if you moved back home and went to school from here. I know your father and Drea would be excited," Victoria beamed.

Lexi listened to her mom rant on and on about school and church for another twenty minutes. She took that time to scroll through all her social media sites, occasionally providing an "un huh.... For real ma" for listening effects.

"Ok baby, I'm going to let you go, I gotta go help your father prepare for tomorrow's services. I'm going to wire you $500.00, I remembered you said you was going shopping earlier," Mrs. Holiday informed her.

"Mom, that won't be necessary. I'm good," Lexi objected.

"Child hush, I love you and I'll talk to you later!" her mom exclaimed. Just like that, her mom ended the call.

Lexi tossed her phone to the side and prepared to get in the shower. She rambled through her top drawer in search of a panty and bra set when she heard her phone vibrating again. Lexi figured it was the notification from Chase Bank, indicating that her mom's hard-headed ass sent the funds anyway, so she just ignored it and headed to the bathroom. She crept down the hallway, trying her best not to wake up Bre who had fallen asleep on the couch. Once she reached the bathroom, she quietly closed the door, cut the water on as hot as she could stand it, and jumped in. The hot water made love to Lexi's body, her perky nipples harden at the sensational touch. She titled her head back and enjoyed the way the H2O was making her feel before grabbing her towel, lathering it up, and washing her body. Lexi washed up three times before turning the water off and carefully stepping on the cream rug in front of her.

After drying off, she wrapped the damp towel around her small frame and exited the bathroom. When she walked past this time, she noticed Bre was no longer laying on the couch, so she peeked her head in the second bathroom where she found her brushing her teeth and washing her face.

"Good morning, beautiful," Lexi said with a smile in which Bre returned.

Lexi then made her way back to her room so she could get her day started. She grabbed the Vaseline Coco Butter lotion off of the dresser, flopped down on the bed, and began to lotion up. She glanced over at her phone, which was lighting up, and grabbed it. She had a missed called from Marcus and a text message from J.R. Of course, she read the text message first and instantly began to blush.

J.R.: Good Morning beautiful. My bad for blowing you off like that yesterday, but I was tied up. Let me make it up to you today, dinner and a movie?

Lexi quickly replied, letting him know they wereall set for later before she continued to get dressed. It was something about J.R., he was unlike the other niggaz she was fucking with. The other men were so attentive to her and her needs, there for her every time she called, but J.R. seemed to never have time for her and for some strange reason, that made her want him even more. The sound of the doorbell ringing made Lexi jump up and grab her robe from behind her bedroom door.

"I got itttttttt!" Bre sang as she passed Lexi's bedroom.

Lexi wondered who the fuck could be stopping by so early and the only person that came to mind was Marcus, but seeing how his car was broke, he wouldn't have had a way. Her suspicions were confirmed when Bre walked in her room carrying a bouquet of red roses.

"Here," she said, tossing the roses on the bed and walking off.

"Damn bitch, what the fuck is your problem?" Lexi questioned as she picked up the beautiful arrangements and read the card that was attached:

"I'M SORRY FOR EVERYTHING, LEXI. I LOVE YOU!"

An instant attitude overcame her as she read those words aloud. The roses were from Randy, one of Lexi's many sponsors. He was a fake drug dealer, turned punk. When they first started talking, he was everything to Lexi, not only did he have that thug appeal that she loved so much, he was generous with his cash flow. However, things took a turn for the worst when he started catching feelings. Luckily one day while they were chilling at his house, one of his exes popped up, Lexi took that situation and ran with it. She was so hurt and couldn't go on talking to him, well at least that's what he thought and ever since that day, he'd been trying to get back into good graces with her. Randy would just deposit money into her account without asking, he was popping up on campus, trying to get her to talk to him, but she was too heartbroken to go on. She had been trying to think of ways to break things off with him for months, but she caught a break when the visitor came by.

Lexi gave the roses one last sniff before carrying them into the kitchen and placing them in the trash. As she headed back to her room, she bypassed Bre in the hallway. Bre intentionally bumped Lexi as if she was trying to dislocate her shoulder.

"Bre, I will fuck you up. You better stop playing with me," Lexi warned.

"FUCK YOU, ALEXIS! I'M SICK OF YOU AND YOUR SHIT. YOU THINK YOU CAN DO WHATEVER

YOU WANT AND I'M JUST SUPPOSE TO...... YOU KNOW WHAT, JUST FUCK IT!" Bre yelled before going into her room and closing the door.

Lexi shrugged her shoulders and continued to her room where she attempted to get dressed for what seemed like the hundredth time. Just as she began to spray her body with her favorite fragrance, Tahiti Island Dream, from Bath and Body Works, Bre came in. Once again, Lexi rolled her eyes before turning around greeting her once best friend.

"Look Lexi, I think we need to talk," she said, taking an uninvited seat on Lexi's California King.

"What up?" she replied nonchalantly.

"I'm tired of arguing with you day in and day out about the same shit," Bre stated.

"That's your fault," Lexi shrugged.

"Why is it always my fault? I don't get it, why must you deal with so many men?" Bre questioned.

"Why is it your concern Bre? I'm not fucking these men and I'm not bringing them here, so I don't get it," Lexi explained.

"Look, I just want my best friend back," Bre said, standing to her feet, walking over to where Lexi was standing.

"Me too, Bre; you know I love you and will do anything for you. I'm sick of arguing, too," she admitted.

"Well, let me make things right," Bre said seductively while licking her lips.

She was now standing directly in front of Lexi, untying the loose knot that was holding her robe together. Alexis allowed her Pink robe to fall to the floor as she began to wonder why she always put herself in fucked up predicaments.

"You know how I feel about you, I just wish you allowed things to be how they are supposed to be and stop worrying about others. Let me love you," Bre said, pushing Lexi backwards until she fell onto the bed.

Lexi's body flopped down while Bre used her legs to pry hers open a little, standing in front of her. Lexi laid back and closed her eyes, she wanted to stop Bre because she knew that was how their friendship became tainted in the first place. Her mind and heart was telling her to end it while her throbbing pussy was begging her to allow her to keep going. Never the one to put up a fight, she allowed Bre's mouth to invade her freshly waxed vagina. She wanted her best friend back, but the way she ate pussy, had her wondering if this could really work.

Chapter 6

Alyssa laid in her bed staring at the ceiling in a daze. She held up her left hand and gazed at the 14K rose gold two carat princess diamond cut ring that was added to her ring finger at dinner the previous night by Corey. She let her hand drop to her side before she returned her focus back to the ceiling and replayed the night before.

Alyssa had just finished applying her make-up when Corey rung her door bell. Dressed in a red sleeveless low cut bodycon dress with a pair of black red bottoms, she answered the door with a smile. When her eyes landed on her man, her juices instantly started to flow. Corey stood at 6' 2" with the complexion of a brown paper bag. His athletic build was covered by an Armani suit that hid his decorated tattooed arms. His jet-black hair was low cut and filled with waves and his pearly whites sparkled every time he flashed his million-dollar smile and the dimple in his right cheek was the icing on the cake.

Alyssa threw her arms around Corey's neck as he pulled her in close, hugging her tightly. Alyssa was 5'5" with cinnamon skin and thick as hell. Her long Brazilian weave stopped at her ass, but she rocked it in a high bun. Her 36 D titties, small waist, and fat ass made niggas mouths drop and her sassy attitude and southern twang added to her charm. Breaking their embrace, Alyssa jogged to her room to grab her black clutch bag and shawl before she locked up her condo and the couple got in the car. They held hands as they drove to the restaurant while they made small talk. The duo arrived at Marea, an expensive Italian restaurant, thirty minutes later. Corey handed his keys to the valet and escorted Alyssa inside the restaurant.

After he gave his name to the hostess, they were escorted to their table and when they reached the table,

Corey helped Alyssa with her chair and when she was seated comfortably, he took his seat on the other side of the table. Seconds later, the waiter came to their table and Corey ordered dinner and drinks for the both of them. When the waiter was out of sight, Alyssa began the conversation.

"Damn, baby. This place is nice as hell," she admired her surroundings. "What you have to tell must be really important," she continued.

"Why you say that?" he chuckled.

"The bigger the news, the more expensive the restaurant. And looking at these prices, I'd say whatever you have to tell me is either really good or really bad, Corey," she smirked.

"Put ya mind at ease sexy because what I have to tell you and ask you is all good. I just hope ya answer to my question is a good one."

"Boy, stop talking in circles and say what you gotta say."

"Alyssa, you know I had a thing for you since our freshman year of college and when I asked you to be my girl, you shot me down because I had too many chicks on my top and you didn't need the drama. I felt some type of way when you rejected me, but I never let it show. After I tore my ACL, all the bitches that were on my top vanished, but you still stood by me and you made a nigga's day when you said you would be my girl when I asked you again the day we graduated. This is the realest relationship I'd ever been in and I want this shit to last forever," he grabbed her by the hand.

"Corey, baby? What are you saying?" Alyssa chuckled nervously.

"Alyssa, will you make me the happiest nigga alive by being my wife?"

Alyssa's mouth hit the floor as she watched her man dig inside his jacket pocket and pull out a ring box. The dazzling diamond ring sparkled in the light when he opened the box and all Alyssa could do was stare at it. With her mouth still gapped opened, she didn't know how to respond to his proposal. There was no doubt that Alyssa loved Corey, and that alone should have made her decision an easy on,e but she had a nagging feeling inside of her telling her not to do it.

"Alyssa?" Corey questioned.

"Yes? I mean yes!" she smiled. "Yes. I'll marry you."

Corey leaned over the table and kissed her lips passionately. He took her hand, put the ring on, and smiled as he gazed into Alyssa's eyes and she did the same. The waiter returned with their drinks and food a few minutes later and the rest of the night was filled with conversation, laughter, and love. The night would have been perfect if the nagging feeling would have subsided after she answered yes to his proposal.

Alyssa took a deep breath before she crawled out of bed, dragging herself into the bathroom to shower. When she was fresh, she got dressed in a pair of light denim True Religion jeans, a light purple Polo sweater, and a pair of wheat colored Timberland boots. Keeping her hair in a bun, she filled her Gucci bag with her wallet, phone charger, and binoculars before she went to the kitchen and fixed a light breakfast. After fixing a bowl of Frosted Flakes, Alyssa rolled her eyes at the sound of the doorbell. She had a feeling that it was her sister. As she looked through the peep hole and saw her sister Anastasia on the other side, she shook her head before opening the door.

"What are you doing here, Stasia?" Alyssa spoke dryly as her sister entered her condo.

"I'm excited to see you too, sis," she rolled her eyes.

"Look, I need you to help me out at the shop today," Anastasia continued.

"Heffa, you must be losing your damn memory. You fired my ass yesterday, remember?" Alyssa closed the door and walked back to the kitchen.

"Shit. That's right," Anastasia followed her sister to the kitchen.

"Even if you didn't fire me, I couldn't help you anyway," Alyssa took a seat at the counter where her cereal was.

"I have something to do," Alyssa continued.

"I'm not even going there with you today, but you are gonna tell me what the fuck is up with that rock on ya finger," Anastasia took a seat at the counter.

"Corey proposed last night," Alyssa answered dryly.

"You don't sound too excited about that, Lyssa. What's wrong?" Stasia quizzed.

"Don't get me wrong now, I love my baby, but I think it's too soon for us to be getting married. I mean we were friends before we became a couple, but I got this feeling in the pit of my stomach that I shouldn't have accepted his proposal," she began to play with her cereal.

"You could just be nervous about becoming a wife and that's normal. Marriage is not something that should be taken lightly and don't let anyone force you into something you really don't want to do," Anastasia honestly replied.

They both glanced at each other knowing the reason behind Anastasia comment.

"Look, don't rush into anything that you're not ready for, aight?" her sister sternly stated.

"Aight sis," Alyssa replied as she stared at her ring.

"Let me get out here. Since I don't have anyone to help me at the shop, I guess I'll have to close it for the day," Anastasia commented as she stood up.

The sisters hugged each other goodbye before Alyssa disposed of her soggy cereal, grabbed her backpack, and rushed out the door. Hopping behind the wheel of her silver 2017 Chevy Impala with tinted windows, she put the car in drive and headed to the Bronx to get some Intel on her subject. Alyssa arrived at her destination forty minutes later and parked on the top of the block that was a known hang out of D'Mani's. She reclined her seat back a little and waited for any signs of her target.

After sitting in her car for almost five hours and still no sign of D'Mani, she called the chief of her team and gave her report for the day. Each member of her team had a location to report to everyday and they were to stake out until they saw any activity. The chief informed her that one of co-workers had eyes on D'Mani on the other side of town and that she could leave her post for the day and to report back the following day, which was cool with Alyssa.

As she drove back home, her mind seemed to wander. Corey's proposal and returning home for the holidays was all she could think about and she was dreading seeing her sisters and parents again. Andrea, her older lawyer sister was a prissy missy/pain in the ass and a daddy's girl, while her baby sister, Alexis, was the mama's girl. The oldest and the baby got most of the attention from their parents which caused Anastasia and Alyssa to become very close. Just the thought of her sitting around the table hearing her parents praise Andrea and Alexis made her angry and that was something she wasn't looking forward to.

"Somebody just shoot me now," she signed as she made her way home.

Chapter 7

When Anastasia woke up the next morning, D'Mani was still on her mind the entire time she showered and got dressed. So much so, that as she prepared breakfast for Kyler, she didn't even hear Richard calling her name.

"Babe," he said placing a hand on her shoulder and finally getting her attention as she scraped the last of the scrambled eggs she was cooking onto a plate.

"What are you thinking about? I've been calling you for the last five minutes," he had a look of concern on his face and somehow instead of her appreciating him caring, it irritated her to no end.

"Sorry, I was thinkin' about work, Rich," she explained dryly, moving away from him so that she could place the plate of eggs and bacon down in front of Kyler where he sat at the table. With her back to Richard, she poured some orange juice into his cup.

"Well, I was thinking about how you've been saying I don't spend any time with you guys, so I figured I wouldn't go in and we'd make it a family day type of thing," Richard cheerfully state.

She froze mid-pour and rolled her eyes.

"I'm actually pretty busy down at the store today," she sighed. "Alyssa already been MIA lately. You know I had to fire her ass yesterday."

"Could you not talk so……urban, Anastasia; especially in front of Kyler," he chastised from behind, causing her to turn to him with a frown. "And I already told you that you should fire her," he continued.

"Are you trying to spend the day with me or you trying to fight?" she tilted her head at him ready for some more dumb shit to come out of his mouth. He was constantly talking about her cursing even though his ass didn't mind anything she said when they were fucking, if you could call it that.

"I'm not trying to fight, Anastasia; it's not like I haven't told you these things on many occasions," Richard said and she couldn't help but roll her eyes.

"And I've told you on plenty of occasions not to talk to me like I'm a child, Richard," Ana spat sizing him up and taking in his appearance. She hoped that he hadn't planned on wearing the light blue collared button up and khaki pants he had on with brown boat shoes, even though she knew he did.

That was his casual look and whenever he wasn't at work that was the type of shit he wore. Not sweats, not slides, not regular tees or timb boots; the man had no swag at all. Anastasia could admit that he was very handsome with his smooth brown skin, thick lips covered by a small mustache, and dark brown eyes. He wore his hair cut so low that he looked almost bald, but surprisingly it fit him well. The thing was, no matter how educated Anastasia was, she was still more attracted to hood niggas than she was to corporate suit wearing ones. That was the problem with Richard. He provided well, had married her and took very good care of her and their son, but he was just a lousy fuck and way too straight laced for her. Plus, he didn't have a back bone. Whenever they argued, he would fold….and fast.

Anastasia wanted a man that would put her in her place sometimes and that's where D'Mani came in. He was everything that Richard wasn't. He definitely gave her that thug love, he had swag out of this world and he didn't let her walk all over him. The only thing was that he wasn't someone she could bring home to her parents. Another thing was the fact that she couldn't trust him. She knew her husband like the back of her hand, she knew that he would take care of home, but with D'Mani just because he claimed he loved her didn't mean that he would always be there. That was the problem with thug ass niggas; they were not dependable, and she couldn't uproot her and her son just to end up left alone, no matter how much she loved D'Mani.

"Honey," he whined and stepped closer wrapping his arms around her. She noted how little she felt when in his arms. There was none of the chemistry or shivers she felt like when D'Mani held her.

"I don't want to fight, I just want the best for you. Cursing isn't ladylike and tracking down a grown woman to work so that she can provide for herself isn't your job," Richard said and kissed the tip of her nose and continued.

"Now, let me take Kyler to school and you can go to the boutique for a couple of hours while I stay here and get some work done. Then, I can swing by and take you to lunch."

"Fine Richard, I'm still going by Alyssa's place first. No matter what you say, that's my sister and I'll always look out for her," she told him matter of factly while folding her arms between them. The look on his face told her that he wanted to say something else, but he kept it to himself.

"Alright Ana," he sighed and gave her a kiss on the cheek before turning to Kyler.

"You ready, bud?"

Anastasia took a moment to look down at their son noticing how quiet he had been all morning. He looked up at his dad and nodded with sadness written all over his face.

"What's wrong, baby?" she couldn't help but ask, wiggling out of Richard's arms and fully facing her baby. Anastasia crouched down to his level and rubbed his cheek affectionately.

"I don't like when you're mad at daddy," he mumbled with his eyes cast down as he pushed food around on his plate.

It broke Anastasia's heart to know that Kyler was noticing how she acted towards his dad. She could feel Richard's eyes on her and knew that he was behind her nodding like a fool. Closing her eyes for a second to try and gather her thoughts, she opened them back up to address him.

"Mommy's not mad at daddy, baby. Sometimes we just don't agree about things, but we still love each other," she tried to explain as best she could.

Honestly, while she wasn't that happy with Richard, she didn't consider that her feelings were so transparent to their son. Most times he was so quiet and in his own thoughts that she didn't even realize he noticed their small spats.

"You just go to school and when you get back, we'll all go out and do something fun," she smiled hoping to put him at ease.

"Okay," he grinned happily and hopped up from his seat at the table to go get his coat and backpack.

Anastasia stood up also facing Richard who had a blank expression on his face. He didn't say anything even though she knew he was dying to.

"Go ahead, Richard. I know you have something to say," she told him, crossing her arms defensively.

"I wasn't going to say anything, Anastasia," he replied with eyes still devoid of emotion. "I agree that we have our disagreements, and I also agree that we love each other. Besides, even though I let you talk big, you know you're nothing without me," he shrugged, placed a kiss on her cheek, and left her there.

It took Anastasia a few minutes to shake off the irritation that had coursed through her at his words. Sometimes Richard acted as though he loved her, then there were the times like these when he made it known that he was aware of the power he possessed. What could she say though, he knew exactly the role he played in her life. So, she sucked it up and grabbed her keys so that she could drop by Alyssa's.

Hours later, after she'd talked to her sister she still wasn't any closer to finding out what was going on with her. Alyssa had told her about her engagement and she was genuinely happy for her, but she knew that something else was going on, she just couldn't put her finger on it. As she sat across from her husband and Kyler, Anastasia felt like she was a thousand miles away. Well, her body was there, but her mind and heart were wherever D'Mani happened to be.

While her son and husband ate their pizza, and talked about their day, she pushed her pasta around on her plate thinking about the last time she'd been able to be with D'Mani. She'd been in a foul mood ever since she had to cancel their plans due to the "family day" and she didn't care who knew it. Of course, he had been upset because this was like the fifth time that in his words "she'd sent him off". It wasn't like she wasn't angry too, but he needed to understand that her family came first. Unfortunately for her, he didn't give her a chance to explain that to him, he just hung up in her face. Anastasia tried to call him back and she also texted, but he just kept leaving her on read. That was one thing you could do to let a person know you didn't give a damn, have those read receipts on and don't reply. At that point, she wasn't even feeling bad about the situation, she was mad at him for being mad and she couldn't wait to give him a piece of her mind.

As if he could hear her thoughts, she looked right up as he entered the door of the restaurant looking good enough to eat. He was rocking a gray skull cap, an army fatigue jacket over a gray hoody, with a pair of dark jeans and some unlaced brown timbs. The only jewelry he had on was a gold Cuban link and a gleaming Rolex, with his signature studs in each ear. As soon as she saw him she could barely breathe and it didn't have shit to do with her lover being in the same room with her husband. It had everything to do with the way her heart skipped when she was in his presence. Trying not to act too obvious she stared a hole in the side of his face, willing him to look back at her. When he finally did look her way, it was as if his eyes went right through her, then just as fast, his attention was elsewhere. She could feel the tears about to burn her eyes as him and a man that was almost dressed similar were led to a table while he continued to ignore her.

"Hey, you okay hun?" Richard asked, looking at her in concern.

"I'm fine, Rich. I think I have an eyelash in my eye. I'll be right back," she lied and hurried off to the bathroom after she'd witnessed D'Mani go in that direction.

Standing out in the small hallway she tried to think of what she would say once he came out. Her palms started sweating and she rubbed them down the sides of her black skinny jeans as she paced.

"Yo, what the fuck you doin' back here, Stasia?" his gritty voice caused her to turn around as he exited the bathroom. She couldn't help but run her eyes up the length of him in awe of how fine he was even though he had a scowl on his face.

"Why aren't you answering my texts, D'Mani? You're getting mad at me when you knew what my situation was the very first day we met."

"And? Shit is different now, a nigga feelins' involved! Yo ass blowin' me off for that Buford ass nigga and you think I ain't gone be pissed," he damn near shouted causing her to look down the hallway to make sure no one heard. Letting out an angry chuckle he began to walk away, but she pulled him right back by the arm of his jacket.

"Don't you walk away from me, Mani! My feelings are involved too, but what am I supposed to do? I'm married!" she hissed as tears fell from her eyes. She didn't think that she would care so much about him, but if she didn't know before she knew now, in this moment, that she didn't want to lose him.

"I know you married, Mrs. Wilson," he said emphasizing her last name. "You better get back to yo family. Richard probably lookin' for you." With that, he walked off leaving her in the hallway in tears.

“Ugh!” she let out a frustrated groan before she sulked into the bathroom to straighten herself up. Once she finally felt like Richard wouldn’t notice she’d been crying, she went back out and sat down at the table while him and Kyler laughed.

“Everything okay babe?” he asked taking in her appearance. Under his scrutiny nervousness kicked in, but D’Mani had already left, so there was nothing to worry about. Putting on a smile she told him.

“Everything’s great, honey.”

Chapter 8

Andrea pulled clothes out of her closet and threw them on the bed, in preparation for her upcoming trip to New York. She wasn't too thrilled about going to New York in November for a conference because it was cold as hell up there, but since two of her sisters were there, Andrea felt like it wouldn't be too bad. She had texted them and told them about her last-minute trip, and they all agreed to at least meet for dinner and drinks. Andrea was only going to be there like a day and a half, so she sucked it up and told herself that it wouldn't be too bad. Her flight was scheduled to leave later on at nine, so that gave her five more hours before takeoff. Since Jackson's airport was small, she didn't plan on leaving home until about 7:30. That would give her enough time to park and get through TSA before her flight even boarded.

After she was satisfied with work and casual attire for her short trip, Drea slipped on a pair of Ugg boots and one of her Tugaloo pullovers and walked next door to her parent's house. She prayed that she wouldn't get lectured about finding a man, getting married, and having some babies, but that seemed to be all her parents talked about every single day. Since she was the oldest and had just celebrated her thirtieth birthday earlier in the year, all her parents talked about was how she should be established by now. She loved and respected them, but low key wished they would leave her alone because she wasn't trying to end up like her sister Anastasia in a miserable marriage.

It wasn't that she hadn't tried, but all of the men that approached Andrea turned out to be losers and she was just over it. Thoughts of moving away consumed her mind a lot, but who would be around to care for their aging parents if she wasn't there. She was already pulling teeth just to get her sister's home for Thanksgiving to surprise their parents. Andrea walked in and went straight to the kitchen where she found her mom cooking.

"Hey mom, where's dad?" she asked as she opened the cake pan and cut a slice of caramel cake.

"You know Abraham is down at the church. He should be back soon," Victoria said as she stirred in a pot on the stove.

"I don't even know why I asked," Drea mumbled and took a bite of her cake.

"You packed and ready for your trip?" Victoria asked.

"Yes ma'am. I finished up before I came over… what you cooking today?" Drea asked.

"Got some neck bones in the crock pot, cornbread and macaroni and cheese in the oven, and these mixed greens in the pot," Victoria replied.

"I'm right on time," Drea said.

"Yeah and you eating dessert before dinner again," her mom chuckled. "You gonna see Anastasia and Alyssa while you up there?" Victoria continued.

"Yes ma'am, we're meeting up tomorrow night. I actually can't wait to see them," Drea said and smiled.

"You be nice… and see if you can find a man up there to marry, so you can give me some grandbabies," Victoria beamed.

"Ugghhh don't start mom. I'm gonna skip dinner and head to the airport if you start this again," Drea rolled her eyes.

"I'm just saying baby… you ain't getting no younger," Victoria fussed.

Andrea rolled her eyes upward and tuned out everything else that her mom was saying. It wasn't like she didn't want all of those things for herself; she just hated to feel pressured into anything just because she was getting older. Andrea had gone out with several men, but none of them measured up to her standards.

"Did you and Lexi have y'all's daily talk this morning?" Andrea cut her mom off and asked, in hopes that she would drop the current irrelevant topic.

"You know I did… she doesn't miss a morning calling. I'm so proud of my baby. I wish she would come home for Thanksgiving since she didn't make it this summer, but she said she bought a ticket to go to New York to see somebody name Jaycee," Victoria said.

"It's Jay- Z, mom," Andrea chuckled.

"We should go visit her soon," Drea added.

"You know I don't like all that traveling. Hopefully, we can all get together as a family real soon. It's been so long since I had all of my babies under one roof," Victoria sadly remarked.

Hearing the sadness in her mom's voice made Andrea that much more adamant about making sure her sisters came home for Thanksgiving. Even if they only came for one day, it would make their parent's happy, but she hoped that they wouldn't be that damn trifling and come all the way home for such a short period of time.

"Hey baby girl!" Abraham sang as he came into the kitchen.

"Daddyyy… heyyy! I thought I was gonna miss you before I left for my trip," Andrea squealed as she got up and hugged her dad.

"Is that today? I'm glad I came on back because it slipped my mind," Abraham said as he scratched his head.

"Daddy, you know you been forgetting stuff lately," Drea noted.

Andrea ended up eating and talking to her parents, and cleaning up for almost three hours. When her dad prompted her to get up and leave before she missed her flight, Andrea finally headed home. When she made it inside, the sound of her cell phone ringing made Andrea finally remember that she didn't take it with her, which was highly unlike her. Andrea normally kept her phone near her at all times. She only planned on visiting with her parents for a few minutes, but just like always, it turned into hours. By the time Andrea grabbed her phone, it had stopped ringing. She looked and saw that it was her best friend that had FaceTimed her and she also had a few missed calls from people who weren't important, so she ignored them and called Hannah back.

"I hope the reason you didn't answer the phone was because you was laid up with a man," Hannah teased right when she answered the phone.

"Not today, bitch… not today. I just got mom off my back," Drea said and rolled her eyes.

"You know… I know she be on your case, but I'm starting to agree with her.

Your ass is just too damn picky," Hannah fussed.

"It's been almost three years since you been laid, boo… have some fun. Just because you fuck somebody don't mean you gotta marry em or have a baby. Just have some fun at least," Hannah continued when Andrea didn't reply.

"I'm about to hang up on your ass," Andrea finally got a word in.

"If you hang up on me, Ima come kick your ass," Hannah chuckled

"I'll be at the airport by the time you make it," Drea said and stuck up her middle finger.

"Oh, your trip is today… girl, just fuck a fine man in New York and get yo life!" Hannah laughed.

"Byyeee hoe!" Andrea said and hung up on her crazy ass best friend.

As soon as she sat the phone down, a text message came through and she knew that it was Hannah cussing her out.

Hannah: Bitch, you lucky you bout to leave, but I'll see you when you get back. Have fun and get some New York dick! ☺

Andrea didn't even bother replying to her best friend and she had her read receipts on. She had met Hannah her freshman year in high school and they had been friends since then. The two of them had gone through the most together and always had each other's backs. Hannah was more of a free spirit until her fiancé, Chad, put her on lock. Hannah always encouraged Andrea to have some fun like she did before getting into a serious relationship.

"Ima shock her ass one day," Drea mumbled as she walked into her room and started grabbing her things.

It was almost one' clock eastern time when Andrea landed in New York after a short thirty minute layover in Atlanta. She was thankful that she didn't have to go to a different gate or else there was no way she would have made her connecting flight in Hartfield's big ass airport. After Andrea got her luggage from baggage claim, she pulled her phone out and requested an Uber. Two minutes later, her phone rang and the diver told her that he was outside in a black Tahoe. Andrea made her way outside and found him near the taxi area. The brisk air hit Andrea suddenly and caused her to shiver. She was glad that she had thought ahead and dressed for the weather. Andrea made it to Raven Hotel about twenty minutes later and checked into her suite. It was located right across from Queensbridge. The conference was only three miles away and was scheduled to start at 9:00 a.m., so Andrea had almost seven hours to spare.

At 7:30 a.m., the sound of the iPhone alarm woke Andrea up. Not being one to hit the snooze button, she got on up and handled her hygiene. Fifteen minutes after eight, Andrea was dressed in a charcoal grey Armani pants suit with black pumps and was headed down to the lobby. She grabbed a bottle of water and a banana from the breakfast bar after requesting an Uber, and waited for its arrival. Once her ride arrived, Andrea hoped in, then texted her sisters in a group message to confirm their date for later that evening. She didn't expect either of them to reply right away, but to her surprise, Anastasia responded almost instantly. Andrea knew that Alyssa would go along with whatever Anastasia said, so it didn't matter if she replied or not, she would be there.

Five o'clock couldn't come fast enough. Even though the seminar was very interesting, Andrea was happy that it was over and glad that the next day was only four hours. She had three hours before it was time to meet up with her sisters. They were meeting at Penthouse 808 which was actually on the rooftop of the Ravel Hotel, so all Andrea would have to do was take the elevator up. There was no need to call them anymore, and since they had been fed well at the seminar, Andrea wouldn't have to eat anything until later that night.

By nine o'clock, Andrea was pissed off sitting at a table all alone in the lounge. Neither Anastasia nor Alyssa were answering her calls or texts. It was one thing to be late, but to be late and not give any type of warning was just rude as fuck. Andrea wasn't a big drinker, but she was on drink number four and ready to order another Long Island Iced Tea.

"You look as pissed off as I am, but you better slow down on the drinks, sexy," a man said as he sat down right across from Andrea.

"I'm good and grown," Andrea slurred a little and took another sip of her drink.

When she finally looked up and locked eyes with the man that sat before her, her heart fluttered and her pussy began to tingle. She was staring at one of the finest men that she had seen in a long ass time. What conflicted her was the fact that he wasn't even a man of her type, but the way that she was feeling just by looking at him had her getting wetter by the second. When he licked his lips and smirked, she knew right then and there that he was a cocky muthafucka.

"You looking at me like I'm a piece of meat or some shit… you want this dick don't you?" the man quizzed.

"Is that how you pick up your hoes?" Drea asked with her head cocked to the side.

The chuckle he let escape his lips let Andrea know that she had hit the nail on the head. At that very moment, the words that Hannah had spoken to Andrea began to ring in her head. The girl who had been taking her drink orders walked over and placed another drink in front of her, and she picked it up and downed it in no time. Andrea looked the stranger in his eyes as she stood up, then motioned for him to follow her. She couldn't believe what she was doing, but the alcohol had given her a lot of courage and she was ready to reach her room before she came to her senses. Hannah told her to get some New York dick, and that was exactly what she did once she made it up to her room, not one, but two rounds and it was indescribable. Andrea didn't even feel bad afterwards that she didn't know the mystery man's name. If she did, she would have flown to New York every weekend just for him to fuck her, but he served his purpose. It would be a one night stand that she would forever remember.

Chapter 9

After the sex escapade with Bre, the both of them laid in the bed and smoked a blunt. Alexis grabbed the remote control off the night stand and turned to her favorite show, *Good Times*. She had a few episodes recorded for times like the present when she just wanted to chill and laugh at JJ's crazy antics. She more so cut it on at the moment because whenever Bre got high, she got into her feelings and hearing her whine and bitch was not on Lexi's to-do-list. Alexis selected to watch the one when Ramona got custody of Penny. She snuggled close to Bre, cut up the volume, and enjoyed her show. As soon as the first commercial came on, Bre started with the bullshit.

"What are you scared of?" she asked, twirling her fingers in Alexis's hair.

Lexi heard her loud and clear, but decided to ignore her.

"LEXI!" she said louder the next time, bass filling her voice.

"Yes honey?" Lexi replied, slightly rolling her eyes.

"I said, what are you so afraid of?" Bre repeated.

"I aint scared of shit," Lexi responded nonchalantly.

"You know what I'm talking about. You confuse me at times. I don't know what we are doing, but what I do know is, I've fallen in love with you and I'm ready to make things official," she confessed.

Lexi let out a loud sigh, she was tired of having the same conversation over and over again with Bre's ass. Unfortunately, English was Lexi's only language, but apparently Bre needed the shit translated in another language.

"Bre, you know I love you to death, but saying that I am in love with you is pushing it. We've been best friends since the third grade, things with us should have never went this far, but it did and that's something I can't take back. Do I enjoy the sex.... Hell yeah, but....."

"So, it's all about sex with you?" Bre cut her off.

"Basically, I mean, I'm not gay," Lexi tried to explain.

"BITCH, PLEASE! YOU JUST AS GAY AS YOUNG M.A......I don't know why you keep trying to convince yourself that you are not. You enjoy when I eat your pussy and you eat mine like a monster, so how the fuck are you straight, Alexis?" she snapped.

Lexi counted to ten in her head, trying her best to avoid going there with her best friend, but Bre was leaving her with no choice. Lexi grabbed the remote that she placed back on the night stand and paused her show. She sat up and scooted to the edge of the bed before turning around and addressing the issue for what seemed like the hundredth time.

"Bre, you really need to chill the fuck out. Like for real my nigga, because I am not trying to be into it with you, but you are leaving me no choice. Look, I'll tell you what, from this day forward, I will not engage in any sexual activity with you. If things don't get better between us, then I will move the fuck out," Lexi snapped back.

Just like clockwork, the waterworks began. Lexi shook her head at Bre who got up and stormed out. Although it pissed her off and irritated the shit out of her that things turned out this way, she couldn't help but blame herself.

"I swear friend, everything gon' be ok.... Fuck him," Lexi said to a crying Bre.

"I mean.... I mean... how can he do me like this?" Bre replied through sniffles.

Lexi rubbed the curly matted weave that sat on top of her best friend since the third-grade head. She tried her best to find the right words to comfort her, but nothing was coming to mind. Bre was heartbroken and although that was something that Lexi had yet to experience, she knew the feeling couldn't be a pleasant one.

"Look Breana, you are a bad bitch and you can get any nigga you want. FUCK TOMMY old dusty ass," Lexi stated.

Everything that she had just said to Bre was the truth, she was indeed a bad bitch. Breana Langley was a Puerto Rican and Black goddess. She had a soft caramel complexion with slanted hazel eyes. A set of full lips that begged to be kissed, two deep dimples that displayed even when she spoke. The sexiest thing about Bre was her natural honey brown hair that hung to the middle of her back and reddish freckles that were scattered across her face. Bre was what you considered "slim thick". She didn't have a big ass booty, but what she did have sat up nicely on her back.

"Look, I know how we gon' get you over that scrub... raise up," Lexi instructed before standing to her feet and heading into the kitchen area of their small dorm room.

Once there, Lexi went inside the blue bin where they kept all their miscellaneous shit and pulled out a fifth of Henny. She then looked over at Bre, waving the bottle in the air smiling.

"What the fuck we finna do with that?" a buck-eyed Bre questioned.

"We finna drink your problems away," Lexi replied, grabbing two cups out of the cupboard.

Bre cracked a smile for the first time all night. She sat up in her twin size bed and waited for Lexi to join her.

"After this, you gon forget all about ummmmmmm what's his face…… see! I forgot about his ass already," Lexi joked, joining her on the bed.

Bre and Tommy had been in an unhealthy relationship since their sophomore year at Jim Hill High School. Although Lexi was never a fan of his, she tolerated him because her best friend loved him to death. After they all graduated, Tommy started acting funny and became very distant. He went away to the University of Connecticut while Bre chose life in the "A." It was Lexi and Bre's freshman year at Clark when Bre stormed through the doors of their dorm room hollering and screaming. Once Lexi finally calmed her down, she described how she was on Facebook and a girl tagged Tommy, along with a picture of an ultrasound, with the caption, "Mommy and Daddy can't wait to meet you." When Bre called him, not only did he not answer the phone, he sent a text message requesting for her to stop contacting him before he blocked her phone number. Bre was devastated, Lexi skipped class to stay with her best friend, trying her best to console her. When that didn't work, Lexi resorted to liquor.

"Neither one of us drink, Lexi. You trying to kill the both of us?" Bre protested.

"Listen, it's Friday. You heartbroken. I'm single. We gon drink this shit and we gon enjoy it," she replied, filling the red Solo cup up to the third line.

"Here. Let's take a shot. I heard it taste better when you drink it fast," Lexi said before downing her cup in one big gulp.

Bre busted out in laughter as Lexi made ugly faces.

"Ohhhh shit.... Bitch it's your turn," she said cheering Bre on.

Once Bre followed Lexi's lead and swallowed hers, Lexi began to pour the both of them other shot. By the time they were on the fourth round, neither of them could stand up.

"Whhhyy a---am I soooo hot?" Lexi words slurred.

"You are not alone.... I am HOT with youuuu. Though you're far awaaayyyy. I am here to stayyyyyyy," Bre sang, struggling to stand to her feet.

Lexi fell back on the bed laughing. When she sat back up, Bre was taking off her shirt.

"Ohhhh let me get my singles," Lexi joked.

"Girl hush, I'm hot," Bre replied, now removing her bra.

"Buuuuttttt... if you want a show, I can give you one," she teased, while she played with her nipples.

Lexi wasn't sure it was the Henny, but her pussy began to throb at the sight of her friend's body.

"Girl, put that little shit up. I don't want to see that," Lexi stated, covering her eyes.

"Girl bye, a mouth full is enough," Bre playfully checked her.

"Mouth full? Bitch where?" Lexi giggled.

"Open your mouth and see," Bre challenged her.

"Ahhhhhhh" Lexi opened up wide, but was caught off guard when Bre held up her part of the bargain and placed one of her breast in her mouth.

At first Lexi was shocked, but it was like her tongue had a mind of its own when it started tracing circles around Bre's hardened nipples. Bre tilted her head back and enjoyed the feeling, letting out soft moans. When Lexi removed her breast from her mouth, Bre grabbed her by the chin, lifting her head up before bending down, placing a soft kiss on her lips. Lexi parted her lips and allowed Bre's tongue to explore her mouth. The two of them engaged in a passionate kiss for about a minute before Lexi relaxed her body on the bed. Bre climbed on top and continued their make out session. About three minutes into it, shit got real when Bre parted Lexi's legs, moved her panties to the side, and began eating her pussy. Lexi figured her mind must have been playing tricks on her because Bre was giving head better than the niggaz she had been with. Unsure if it was the liquor courage or a fantasy that she's always wanted to play out, after Bre made her come effortlessly, she went down on her. She knew that all this was new to her and that she didn't know exactly what she was doing, but she didn't allow that to stop her. She just did all the things that felt good to her, to Bre and it worked. Bre's legs were shaking in no time as the orgasm took over her body.

That was the first time, but it damn sure wasn't the last; which is why Bre was storming out of the room in tears.

Lexi got up from the bed before going down the hall to the bathroom and washing between her legs. She wasn't about to let Bre and her overdramatic ass ruin her day. She still had shopping to do and a date with J.R. Lexi threw on a pair of ripped up jeans, a white baby tee, and her Prada gym shoes. She threw her long weave into a ponytail, grabbed her jean jacket, purse, and headed towards the door. She walked past the kitchen where Bre was, Lexi smirked at the evil look that she got, but proceeded out the door. Before she could make it to her car, she received a text message that made her fume.

Best Friend Bre: I'm glad you think shit funny. I'm glad you think playing with my heart and feelings is a game. BITCH, I GOT YO GAME! I wonder what PASTOR Holiday and the first lady would say when they find out their little perfect baby is sinning beyond alllll sins!!!!

Chapter 10

"Oooh shit, Corey!" Alyssa moaned as he pushed his dick deep inside her.

With her legs on his shoulders, Alyssa's eyes rolled to the back of her head as she enjoyed the dick her man was giving her. Corey grabbed her ankles and increased his pace from a slow medium pace to medium fast. Alyssa continued to moan to the high heavens while Corey focused on the task at hand, which was making her cum for the fourth time. Corey's eight-inch shaft was long and thick and Alyssa handled it like a champ, but sometimes she would run from it so he could fuck her harder, which was what she did.

"What I tell you about runnin' from me?!" he said as he spread her legs apart and rammed his dick into her wetness.

"Oh My God, Daddy!" she moaned.

"Take this dick and stop playin' with me!" Corey demanded.

Alyssa grabbed her ankles, so Corey could continue to fuck her brains out. She loved when he fucked her rough and she tried to keep her eyes open, so she could watch him as he put in work. Moments later, her legs began to tremble and they both knew that her fourth nut was near.

"Go head and let that shit go, so I can bust!" he said and then kissed her lips, which sent her over the edge.

Seconds later, she flooded his dick with her juices as he filled her with his seed. He laid on top of her for a while as their breathing returned to normal. She rubbed his head as they laid there and she was almost sleep until Corey broke the silence.

"Aye, what month do you want to get married in?" he quizzed

"I don't know, Bae. I think I want to get married in the spring. That way it's not too hot or too cold."

"So, you have been thinkin' about our weddin'?" Corey pulled her close and inquired.

"Of course. Why wouldn't I?" she chuckled nervously.

"Because most women be hyped as hell about getting' married and start plannin' shit right away. I haven't heard you say anythin' about it since I proposed and that was days ago. Did you at least tell Anastasia and Kelly?" he pushed himself up and looked at her.

"I told Anastasia the day after. I didn't tell Kelly yet, but I will," Alyssa confessed.

"Are you havin' doubts, Alyssa? Be honest." Corey wanted to know.

"I'm not having doubts, Corey. I'm just nervous about being a wife. That's all," she answered honestly.

"Come on now, Bae. You're already the perfect girlfriend. The only thing that's gonna change is ya title and that we're gonna be on paper. That's it. You're gonna be the perfect wife. You hear me?" Corey lifted her chin and looked her directly in the eyes and proclaimed.

"Yes," she blushed.

"Good because ya ass ain't got no choice, but to marry me," he pecked her lips and stood up.

Alyssa giggled as she watched him walk out the room. She noticed that the sun was starting to rise and wondered what time it was. She snatched her phone off the nightstand to check the time and it was a few minutes before eight. The only thing Alyssa had to do was sit at her usual spot and wait for D'Mani to show his face. Her task seemed boring at times because she had yet to lay eyes on the mystery man, but it beat sitting at the office. He had been to every other spot at least once, except for her location. She couldn't help but think that someone tipped him off, but if that was the case, she figured she'd be dead by now. Alyssa was about to place her phone back on the nightstand until her best friend of five years FaceTimed her. She answered the call and Kelly's face appeared on her screen.

"Wassup Hoe? What you up to?" Kelly asked right away.

"Nothing much. I'm at Corey's right now. What's going on with you?" Alyssa asked.

"I miss you, boo! We need to link up. I get off work at five. We can go to our favorite spot for dinner and drinks," Kelly expressed.

"Sounds like a plan. I got some news that shouldn't be discussed over the phone anyway. I rather tell you in person," Alyssa chattered.

"Aww shit now. Aight. Don't say no more. Save it for later. Bye!" Kelly exclaimed.

She placed her phone on the nightstand and got out of bed making her way to the master bathroom where she found Corey in the shower. Alyssa opened the shower door and stepped inside. He was standing under the shower head facing her and by the way she bit her bottom lip and the expression that covered his face, Corey knew that she wanted to be fucked some more.

"Do you ever get enough of this monster?" he licked his lips.

"Hell nah," she smirked before dropping to her knees.

After fucking in the shower for an hour and a half, they washed up, got dressed and promised to check in before they got in their cars and drove off. Alyssa drove to her location floating on cloud nine. Every time she spent time with Corey, her love for him grew deeper with each passing moment. She loved how they chilled together and watched movies, played cards or she watched him as he played video games. She didn't care what they did as long as they were together and waking up to him in the morning was something Alyssa enjoyed the most. The evening they spent together mixed with the brief conversation about the wedding and the way she was feeling had her ready to marry Corey the following day. Her uncertainty of becoming a wife had slowly subsided and she was ready for the new journey that was waiting for her.

Alyssa arrived at her destination close to an hour later and parked in her usual spot. There was an empty spot in front of her, which gave her the perfect view to see. She noticed a few people coming in and out of the trap spot and took pictures of them. Her spot was popping more than usual, but even with all the traffic that was coming to the spot, there was still no sign of D'Mani. She jotted down everything she saw and took pictures of everybody that came through the block.

When four o'clock rolled around, the activity on the block had died down some, but she had gathered enough information to report to the chief. She placed her earphones in her ear and called her boss as she drove down the block. He was pleased with the information he received and she informed him that she would text him the pictures she took when she got home and ended the call. When she arrived at her condo, she rushed to her room to change her clothes, shoes, and to fix her hair before she went to meet her friend at their favorite restaurant. Alyssa texted the pictures she took to her boss before she grabbed her jacket and purse, then left out her house, locking the doors behind her.

The Manhattan traffic was hectic, but Alyssa still made it to Butter, her favorite restaurant, by five thirty that evening. The valet helped her out the car and handed her a ticket before she switched inside. When the host saw her coming, she grabbed two menus and escorted her to her favorite table, which was a booth on the right-hand side of the restaurant. Alyssa took off her jacket when she reached the table and didn't bother to look at the menu.

"I'll let Miss Baxter know you're here when she arrives," the host smiled before he walked off.

Alyssa retrieved her phone from her purse and saw that she had a text from Kelly saying that she was ten minutes away and to order her usual. She replied okay and decided to text Corey.

Alyssa: Hey baby. Wyd?

Corey: I just got finished doin' a taping for this show. I'm about to link up with my cousin in a few. What you up to, shawty?

Alyssa: At Butter waiting for Kelly.

Corey: Aww shit. Let me get y'all bail money ready now.

Alyssa: LOL. Shut up. We're going to be good, bae.

Corey: You ain't gotta lie, lyssa. Lol. Anyway, what you got planned for Thanksgivin'?

Alyssa: My oldest sister called and said she wanted me to come home for the holidays. So, that's what we're doing.

Corey: Are you sure that's what you wanna do? You know you and the fam don't get along like that.

Alyssa: I know, but I want you to meet my family. No matter how fucked up we may be.

Corey: Aight sexy. Well talk about that later on. I'll be at ya crib no later than midnight.

Alyssa: Okay. Behave yourself.

Corey: I don't want nobody else but you, Love.

She couldn't help but laugh as the lyrics to her favorite Trey Songz hit entered her mind. The waiter came over and she gave him the food and drink orders. A couple of minutes later, Kelly entered the restaurant and walked in her direction. Alyssa stood to her feet and greeted her friend with a big hug.

Alyssa and Kelly met their freshman year at a get together that was for freshmen only. Kelly was whooping ass at the ping pong table and after her fourth straight win, she needed a new opponent. Alyssa was glued to her phone when Kelly asked her to play her. Alyssa refused at first, but after Kelly called her punk for not accepting the challenge, she got up and took her place at the table. After Alyssa beat Kelly two games out of three, Kelly had a new-found respect for her and they had been tight ever since. Kelly was born and raised in Philly and had a feistiness about her that drove men crazy and had a body to match. She was the same height and weight as Alyssa and only a few shades darker. Alyssa and Kelly had helped each other through their toughest times at college and promised to have each other's backs until the day they died. The bond that they had created had been solid for a few years and seemed to be growing stronger as the time went on.

"Damn girl! It's so good to see you!" Kelly broke their embrace and they sat down at the table.

"Yes, it is. The last time I saw you was like a month ago," Alyssa thought back.

"Yeah, man. This new job keeps me going. Working for a fortune five hundred company is busy work. I'm trying to be like my girl, Taraji P Henson, in that movie *Think Like a Man*," Kelly explained.

"I know that's right. Keep going hard like you've been doing and you'll be the CEO in no time," Alyssa affirmed. They high fived each other.

"Bitch, what the fuck is that on your finger?" Kelly grabbed her left hand to get a better look at the rock on her finger.

"Oh, that? That's just my engagement ring," Alyssa giggled like a school girl.

"Get the fuck out of here! Corey popped the question for real?" Kelly queried.

"He sure did, Kels!" she beamed.

"I'm so happy for you, Boo! Congratulations!" Kelly bubbled.

"Thanks, girl," Alyssa thanked her as she admired her ring for the hundredth time.

"Who else knows about y'all engagement?" Kelly asked.

"Just you and Anastasia. Corey and I are going to my parents' house for the holidays and I'll announce my engagement there," Alyssa said.

"You're actually going home? Who called you? Andrea?" Kelly asked.

"You know she did. She told me I was coming home and I wasn't trying to argue with her." Alyssa rolled her eyes. "You know Mississippi is the last place I want to visit, but I'm going home to spend time with my parents'. I'm going to try my best to play nice with my oldest and baby sister, but if they start any shit, it's on," Alyssa clarified.

"Just try to make the best of it and if you think some shit is about to pop off, just remember that you're there for your parents. If that don't work, make sure you and Anastasia tear they asses up," Kelly concluded.

They burst into laughter and seconds later, the waiter returned with their food and cocktails. The ladies made a toast to their friendship and dug into their food. Alyssa wanted to let her friend know that she was working for the FBI, but decided that she needed to keep that under wraps for the time being. She didn't want her best friend to look at her sideways because she was working with the feds. She knew Kelly wouldn't judge her, but she didn't want to compromise her mission.

After three drinks, a full dinner, and dessert, the ladies decided to call it a night. Alyssa promised that she would keep in touch with her bestie when she got ready to start planning the wedding. Kelly threatened to beat her ass if she didn't uphold her promise. After Kelly congratulated her again and told her how happy she was for her, they hugged and parted ways. Alyssa handed the valet her ticket and he quickly came back with her car. Jumping behind the wheel, she slowly pulled out of the parking lot to avoid hitting anybody and when she was on the street, she sped home. When she arrived home, she undressed, took a hot shower, and climbed in the bed. Alyssa sent a text to Corey letting him know that she was waiting on him. He replied telling her that he would be there soon. She smiled as she got comfortable in bed and waited for her man to arrive.

Chapter 11

It had been a couple of days since Anastasia had seen D'Mani while she was out with her family. She had tried to see where he was coming from, with this attitude, but she couldn't understand. He knew from day one that she had a family; hell, one of the first things out of her mouth had been that she was married. For him to get upset with her about some shit she couldn't and wouldn't change was beyond her, but Anastasia couldn't pretend like she didn't miss him. Which was why she found herself driving over to his house after he'd ignored damn near twenty calls and texts.

As soon as she pulled up, she saw his car parked in the driveway and another car right behind it. Anastasia found herself getting pissed off at the thought of him being laid up with some bitch while he ignored her damn calls. She angrily slammed her car door shut and stumped up the sidewalk in her six-inch nude, red bottoms. The white and tan pencil skirt that she wore made it difficult to walk at a fast pace, but somehow, she managed to climb the stairs to his house in record time. She held down the doorbell and tapped her foot against the stone porch.

"D'Mani! Open this god damn door!" Anastasia hollered loudly not caring about his neighbors or the bitch he had in there. She was just about to start yelling again when D'Mani snatched the door open and peered down at her angrily. He was looking damn good as he stood before her shirtless in just a pair of black basketball shorts, black ankle socks, and some Nike slides. Anastasia momentarily lost her voice looking at him standing there looking like a straight full course meal.

"Anastasia, what the fuck is you doin' comin' over here yellin' and ringin' my damn bell?" he spat with his face full of irritation as he looked around to make sure she hadn't disturbed his neighbors.

"Why you not answerin' the fuckin' phone D'mani? You got a bitch up in here?" she finally found her voice and tried to get past him and into the house. He easily blocked her entrance which only further pissed her off.

D'Mani grabbed her roughly by the arm and pulled her closer to him and gave her the death stare.

"I let you get away with a lot of shit ma, but if you keep showin' yo ass out here I'ma fuck yo lil ass up!" he seethed.

It was something about the way he was looking at her that let her know that he meant business. Anastasia took a deep breath and tried to get herself together. She knew she didn't have a right to come over to his house acting a fool, but she couldn't help herself. Even though she had no intentions on leaving her husband for him, she couldn't deny her feelings. It seemed that in D'Mani's mind the decision should have been easy for her to make if she loved him like she claimed, but things just weren't that clear cut.

"Damn what's takin' yo ass so long?" Anastasia's eyes landed behind D'Mani, where another woman stood dressed almost identical to him in a tank top and some of his basketball shorts with no shoes or socks on. She had a game controller dangling from her fingers which sort of put Anastasia at ease, but just because they hadn't been fucking at the moment didn't mean that they hadn't. It had been days since she had talked to him and it was no way that the only reason he had ignored her was because he was mad. Looking at the brown skinned cutie standing behind him, Anastasia instantly knew she was the reason behind him disappearing on her. Tears began to cloud her eyes even though she willed herself not to cry. Her eyes fell on D'Mani as he stood there silently and she didn't even give him a chance to say anything before snatching her arm away.

"You know what, you don't have to worry about me anymore, D'Mani. Go ahead back to your guest." She told him ready to make a dramatic exit. She knew she had no right to be upset, but he'd just told her his feelings were involved and days later there he was with another woman. Sure, she was confused about her feelings and she wasn't ready to leave her husband for him, but she did love him.

Anastasia started for the stairs, but was quickly snatched back by D'Mani.

"Where the fuck you goin', Stasia?" he barked holding her close to his body as she struggled to get free.

"I'm goin home! I don't have time for this shit, D'mani!" she fought against him holding back her tears. It truly took everything in her not to melt into his arms. He smelled so good and she closed her eyes and tried to shake the urge to give in.

"Calm yo ass down Stasia, damn! That's my fuckin' cousin, Narelle!" he explained still trying to stop her from fighting him off. At the word cousin, she stilled. She couldn't help but wonder if he was just saying that to stop her from leaving. Who was she kidding though, if she didn't know shit else about D'Mani, she knew that he wasn't a liar.

With her back still to him as he gripped both of her arms above her elbows and close to her body, she turned her head slightly.

"I swear it's my cousin, ma…. I'm mad about you wantin to stay in that fuck ass marriage, but I'm not tryin' to hurt you," he told her in a quiet tone and placed a soft kiss on the side of her neck.

Once the tension left her body, he loosened his grip on her arms, allowing her to turn around.

"Come inside so we can talk, it's cold as fuck out here," he said.

After she nodded her head, Anastasia let him lead her back into the house where the girl, Narelle, stood in the doorway; the game remote was gone and replaced with a bag of Doritos. It was obvious she'd been standing there watching what was going on.

"Nana, what yo ass doin' with that big ass bag of chips, man?" D'Mani asked as we stepped inside and closed the door behind us. Anastasia watched while she gave him a cheesy grin and licked her finger.

"Shit, I was just watchin' the show," she shrugged, then tucked the bag of chips, so that she could hold out a hand to Anastasia.

"Hey, I'm his cousin, Narelle," she smiled as the two shook hands. Lust filled her eyes as she held onto Anastasia's hand and looked over her body from head to toe.

"Hell nah, Narelle get yo hands up off my shorty!" D'mani laughed, removing Anastasia's hand causing her eyes to widen.

"What? She fine as hell," she shrugged again and winked at Anastasia, blowing her a kiss.

"Maaaan get yo ass on," Hh told her, playfully waving her off while ushering Anastasia towards the stairs. She walked off laughing and Anastasia looked to D'mani for confirmation that Narelle was gay. He nodded with a smirk on his face making her feel even more dumb than she'd felt when he told her that was his cousin.

"D'Mani, we could have talked downstairs, we ain't need to come up here," she told him with little conviction, already knowing what he was thinking and silently craving it. Never stopping his stride to his bedroom, he continued to plant kisses along her neck and shoulders, adding a little tongue just as they reached the door.

"Tell that shit to somebody else, Stasia. I know exactly what you came over here for…and it for damn sure wasn't to talk," he whispered, ignoring her weak attempt at telling him no, while his hands roamed her body igniting heat all over her.

She threw her head back as he sucked the spot just behind her ear while pulling her skirt up around her waist. He grazed his fingers across her bare sex, and nipped at her earlobe. grunting when he realized that she didn't have any panties on.

"Yeah, you was tryna get real nasty for daddy, huh?" he asked and pushed her further into the room with a thrust of his hips. She could feel her wetness running down her legs and he hadn't even really touched her yet. With a low moan, she grinded her ass against his hardness as he shut the door behind them.

"D'Maniiiiii," she whimpered as he ran his hands along her body intentionally avoiding her throbbing center. When he got her over to the bed he finally spread her lips and slipped a finger inside.

"Damn…you wet as fuck!" he growled before bending her body over the bed.

His dick poked straight at her opening when he freed himself of his shorts and he eased inside of her slowly. With one leg propped up on the bed, he leaned over her body and pulled her bra and top down, squeezing her breasts in each hand. Anastasia pressed her face into his plush black and gold quilt, feeling herself on the brink of an orgasm already. She arched her back and tried to match his strokes, winding her hips like she was an island girl, but he put a stop to that fast. Lifting himself up, D'Mani grabbed her hips and quickened his pace.

"Nah ma, I'm runnin this show!" he told her, smacking her on the ass hard. Anastasia yelped in pain and pleasure as her stomach got tight and her head began to spin.

"Mmmm…dammnnn, D'mani!" she groaned, grabbing the blanket with both hands, while her body shook preparing to release.

"You ready to let that pussy rain?"

"Yessss daddy," Anastasia couldn't stop her eyes from rolling into the back of her head.

"Let me feel you then," his voice was raspy as he dug deep into her guts and her cream coated his dick.

Her cries echoed through the room as she came and her body went limp, even though she knew D'Mani was nowhere near done. Just as she expected, he didn't give her but a few seconds to rest before tapping her thigh and lifting her up. On wobbly legs, she stood to her feet and faced D'Mani. He let out a chuckle, then sank his teeth into his lips while he devoured her with his eyes.

"Take that shit off, ma!" he ordered, taking a step back and slipping out of his own clothes only to hop on the bed right after.

Anastasia felt drunk off the dope dick he'd just delivered, she stumbled a little as she tried to come out of the tight skirt and top that she wore. She was damn near about to fall over when D'Mani reached out and pulled her between his legs by her bunched up skirt.

"Let me help."

He hooked his thumbs into the waistband, eased the skirt over her hips, and slid it the rest of the way down her body until it landed in a heap on the floor. She grabbed ahold of his shoulders to steady herself as she lifted each foot and stepped out of her clothes and closer to him. D'Mani stood up with her with his hands still on her body, he grazed them underneath her shirt and helped her out of that too, throwing it across the room. She wasn't ready when he pulled her onto the bed on top of him, his pretty brown dick standing between the both of them.

"Gone head, like daddy taught you," he looked up at her through his thick lashes, with nothing but lust in his eyes.

Anastasia just had to kiss those juicy lips he kept licking. She leaned down teasing his dick, sliding it between her lower lips while she sucked his bottom lip into her mouth. They explored each other's tongues while she grinded against him, until she finally couldn't take it anymore. Like he was meant to be there, he slipped right inside of her with a small thrust and she moaned loudly.

"Mmmmm," she lifted herself up and planted her hands against his chest as she winded her hips on top of him. D'Mani pinched her left nipple while he put the other into his mouth and twirled his tongue around it, before releasing it with a loud smack.

"Damn ma," he mumbled, pulling her face to his for another kiss.

Anastasia could feel herself on the verge of another orgasm and she squeezed him with her pussy muscles.

"Ahhhh… I'm bouta cummmm," she cried, throwing her head back and bouncing up and down on his dick.

"Let that shit go then, baby!" D'Mani grunted like he was about to lose control himself.

As usual, her body gave in to his demands and she came long and hard. He held her with one hand on her shoulder and thrust himself into her two more times before spilling his seeds deep inside of her. They both sat stuck in the same position, unable to move after all that. Anastasia laid her head on his shoulder trying to catch her breath. D'Mani laid back in bed, so that they could get more comfortable and they must have fallen asleep because the sound of D'Mani's phone brought her back to reality.

She sat straight up and looked around until her eyes landed on the clock that sat next to his bed. The time read half past twelve and she cursed under her breath, before waking D'Mani. He groaned in his sleep and opened each eye slowly.

"What? What's up?" he quizzed.

Anastasia quickly got off the bed and began to run around pulling on her clothes in a rush, while he sat up on the edge of the bed watching her with his face full of irritation.

"I have to go! I'm late, D'mani!" she said hysterically.

"That's what the fuck you woke me up for? So, you could run yo ass back to that nigga?" his voice was still a little croaky from just waking up, but Anastasia could still hear the anger in it. She stepped into her heels and turned to him as she buttoned her shirt.

"D'Mani, you know I have to go..." she tried to explain, but he shook his head not even trying to hear her out.

"I didn't, but I damn sure do now!" She watched as he stood and put his shorts back on with his back to her.

"Don't be that way... I.... I just need some time," she pleaded, touching his shoulder, but he shrugged her off and fixed a cold stare on her.

"Nah, I'm good on you, ma. You want yo family to work out gone head, but I ain't bouta be sittin' over here waitin on you to figure that shit out," he said nonchalantly.

Anastasia wanted to say something.... anything, but her words were stuck in her throat, and the way he was looking at her showed that he had no interest in shit she was saying. Blinking to keep her tears at bay, she gave him a single nod and rushed out of his house without another word.

When Anastasia got to her house, she was surprised to see Richard's car still there. She had over five missed calls from him and she figured that he would have just gone back to the office since she wasn't home for them to meet for lunch. Taking a deep breath, she stepped out of her Lexus truck and tried to shake off her nerves. The last thing she wanted to do was run into Richard with D'Mani's scent basically coming off of her pores, but she would figure something out. She paused when she realized her friend Lizzette's car was parked out front and her eyes traveled from her car to the house twice before she shrugged and kept it moving. Her messing around with D'Mani had her so damn paranoid that she was questioning if her friend, who was married with her own little piece, had been fucking her boring ass husband. She shook her head at how crazy it was to even think that and started up the walkway to the stairs when Lizzette breezed out of the front door. The look of shock at seeing her was missed to Anastasia and she continued up to where she stood on the porch greeting her as usual.

"Hey boo," she gushed blowing an air kiss Lizzette's way. She admired the black Prada dress she wore, with matching shoes.

"Oh, hey girl, I was just in there looking for you," she laughed as she stared at Anastasia's appearance, then a sneaky smile crept on her face.

"So, you went and got your fix?" she smirked.

Lizz knew all about D'Mani. They'd been friends since Anastasia and Richard had moved there and started working at the same firm as her husband. Anastasia knew that she could trust her though because Lizz had her a man, too. Anastasia hadn't met him, but she'd met her husband and although he was fine as hell for a white guy she knew he wasn't breaking Lizz's back out.

"Girl shhhhh," Anastasia looked at her like she was crazy, then to the door.

"Aw girl, Richard ass ain't heard nothin'. We were waitin' on you and drinkin' coffee, and now he upstairs shittin' it out," she laughed and waved Anastasia off.

"Right, well I'll call you tomorrow and maybe we can go shopping or something, you still got that nigga credit card, too?" Anastasia asked her. Even though she hadn't met the man she knew everything about him besides his name, but whoever he was he took damn good care of Lizz.

"For sure, it sure as hell ain't nothin going on at my house," Lizz complained with a slight frown, but it quickly disappeared replaced by her gorgeous smile.

Lizz had to be one of the most attractive women Anastasia had run across since they had been in New York and she wasn't just exaggerating because it was her friend. She stood 5'5" with a light complexion and had beautiful dark green eyes. One would never know that she had black in her had it not been from the confession during conversations.

"Okay, I'ma talk to you later! Bye boo!" she said, walking briskly off the porch and to her car.

Anastasia gave her a final wave before heading into the house and straight to the kitchen. Since Richard's ass was in the bathroom, there was no way she could just go in there to take a shower without him wondering why. As soon as she passed their refrigerator, she backtracked to the coffee that sat on the kitchen island. Without giving herself a chance to change her mind, she threw the whole cup on her dress knowing that she would probably never be able to get it cleaned. She let out a breath of frustration and a quiet RIP to her skirt before turning and marching up the stairs and into their bathroom.

Richard sat on the toilet with a Reader's Digest in his lap and she almost wanted to smack that shit out of his hands. He looked up at her and rolled his eyes, before closing the magazine and sitting it on the sink.

"Where have you been, Anastasia?" he demanded, grabbing the roll of tissue.

"First of all, what we are not about to do is discuss anything while you're on the toilet wiping your ass," she said through gritted teeth, disgusted that he thought it would be okay for him to do that.

"We'll talk about whatever I want after I took time out of my busy schedule to come take you to lunch and you weren't even here and didn't have the decency to answer my calls!" his voice got louder and he prepared the tissue to wipe himself.

"You know what, I just got in the damn house, Richard and as you can see, I spilled a whole damn cup of coffee on myself trying to avoid getting in an accident! That's what took me so long!" she lied, matching his glare before starting the shower.

He finished his business and she frowned at the fact that he didn't even wait for her to get in the shower. After he flushed, he washed his hands and tried to approach her as he dried them looking guilty for snapping at her. Anastasia held a hand up to stop him from coming any closer. She checked the temperature of her water, then began to peel the wet skirt and shirt away from her body. The last thing she needed was him coming anywhere near her until she was smelling a little more like Anastasia and a little less like D'Mani.

"You don't even want a quickie before I have to go back to work?" he hinted with his brows raised. She gave him a nasty look and shook her head.

"I'm really not in the mood, Richard; especially after having to see you wipe your ass," she snapped and stepped into the shower closing the door on him and any conversation he was trying to have. He stood outside the shower for a minute or so looking dumb as hell, until he finally left out of the bathroom and eventually the house, slamming the front door behind him.

Chapter 12

Two days had passed since Andrea had returned from New York, and ninety-nine percent of the time she had been thinking about the night that she shared with the mystery man.

"Follow me," Andrea said and turned her glass up one more time being sure not to leave any of the liquid courage behind.

Hannah's words kept ringing in her mind, and the tingling sensation she felt between her legs gave her enough courage to head to the elevator and hit the button for the sixth floor. Anastasia and Alyssa always called Andrea 'miss goody two shoes' and she briefly wondered how they would feel if they knew what their big sister was about to do. The thought quickly left her mind because there was no way in hell that she would ever tell their ungrateful asses. The fine specimen of a man was right behind her, and she knew that he had to be just as horny as she was.

When the elevator chimed alerting them that they had made it to their designated floor, Andrea pulled her room key out of her clutch. As soon as she opened the door and went inside, the man wasted no time taking control of the situation. Andrea was a BBW by the American status, but she wore it well. Her wide hips automatically put her in a size sixteen bottoms, but her flat stomach, size 36D cups, and confidence allowed her the ability to give any model a run for their money. The way that her man for the night picked her up, you would have thought that she only weighed a buck fifty.

"Yeah, I can tell you need some dick in ya life," he stated as he picked Andrea up and roughly threw her on the bed.

Surprisingly, instead of the shit making her mad, it turned her on. Andrea licked her lips as he removed his shirt and revealed his tatted frame. She knew that she was in the presence of a thug. If it had been any other occasion, Andrea would have been running away from him like Forest Gump, but she was willing to go through one night to fulfill one of her secret fantasies. She figured why not since she would never see him again. Instead of just lying there gawking, Andrea decided to remove her clothes. By the time that she was done, her partner was as well and she laid there frozen as she stared at his big ass, monster dick.

"Don't get scared now. I ain't gon hurt ya baby," he smirked.

Before she could reply, he had towered over her and began kissing her sensually, silencing any words that threatened to leave her mouth. By far, it was the best kiss that Andrea had ever had in her whole thirty years of existence. He rotated between rough and gentle and Andrea just knew that there had to already be a puddle on the sheets beneath her. As he made his way down, she didn't expect him to lick the kitty, but he did just that and more. The skillfulness of his tongue caused Andrea to cum two times. She tugged at the sheets as he feasted on her and just knew that the neighbors heard her cries. If she had known his name, they definitely would have known as well.

Andrea was fully prepared to return the favor since he had blessed her with the best head that she had ever received in life, but before she could do so, she heard him fumbling with a wrapper and shortly afterwards, he was entering into her wetness.

"Damn! You tight as fuck!" he expressed as he slowly slid his thickness inside of her as she winced in pain.

When Andrea looked up, his eyes were rolled to the back of his head, and when he finally opened them, the look that she saw in his eyes made her heart flutter. She briefly wondered what if they had met on different terms, but when she finally relaxed and was able to take in his size, she began to enjoy everything that he was giving her.

"Oh, my gawwddd," Andrea moaned as he worked her over.

"Tell me to fuck this pussy," he demanded and Andrea ignored him. "I... said... tell... me... to... fuck... this... pussy!" he gritted between pumps.

"Shiiitttt... fuck this pussy!" Drea succumbed.

She figured that since she obliged, it gave him an extra boost because out of nowhere, he flipped her over and swiftly entered her from the back. He tugged at her Brazilian weave, and Andrea didn't have one fuck to give because of the way that he was making her body feel. As she began to throw the pussy back on him, she felt his body language as it began to stiffen and knew that he was about to cum.

"Cum wit me," Andrea told him, and just like that, they both came and fell onto the bed.

No words were spoken as they laid there. Andrea didn't have any regrets about what had just transpired. She actually felt liberated. After a couple of minutes had passed, he got up and went into the bathroom. Andrea heard the water running, so she knew that he was cleaning himself up. A few minutes later, Drea looked up and saw him walking back out. Even though his dick wasn't hard, it was still huge and caused Andrea to salivate. She sat up and pulled him to her before he could put his clothes on. Andrea took him into her mouth. She gagged at first, but after a few minutes, she had him moaning the way that he had her sounding just moments ago. When his dick began pulsating in her mouth, she felt satisfied and pushed him down onto the bed. She eased down onto his hardness and they both hissed. Andrea enjoyed riding the hell out of his dick and after they came again, she wished that she could pack it up and take it with her.

"I better get my ass outta here before I fuck around and wanna marry that good ass pussy you got... damn!" the man said and Andrea smirked.

"Yeah, that's a good idea because you got me wanting to take that dick back home wit me," she smiled.

Once he was fully dressed, Andrea got up so that she could go and take a shower. Several thoughts popped into her head, but she decided that it was best to leave well enough alone. Before he walked out, he looked into Andrea's eyes and she felt like he was reading her mind.

"I know you ain't never done no shit like that before. That ain't even you, but I'm glad you did, ma," he said and exited without another word being spoken.

"Helllοooo… earth to Drea!" Hannah said while clapping, which immediately broke Andrea from her reverie.

"Damn… stop yelling girl," Andrea fussed.

"I mean, yo ass was sitting there forever just smiling and shit. Fill me in, so I can smile, too," Hannah said.

They were sitting at The Iron Horse Grill on lunch break catching up with each other. Andrea didn't have to be in court until the next day, so after lunch, her evening would consist of going over the case and prepping. She took a sip of her water and wondered exactly how she was going to fill her best friend in on what took place in New York. She knew that Hannah would be excited just because she finally got some, and she wasn't a judgmental person at all, but Andrea was conflicted because even though it was only supposed to be one night, she found herself wanting to search for the mystery man.

"I did it!" Drea confessed.

"You did it? Like did IT? When? Where? Was it good? Give me details!" Hannah rambled.

"I got some New York dick like you said," Drea blushed.

"Oh, my gawd! Tell me what happened," Hannah gave her friend her undivided attention.

Andrea began by telling her friend how her sisters ditched her and she hadn't heard from them since before she arrived in New York. It reminded her that she hadn't cussed them out for it yet, but Andrea made a mental note to take care of that face to face when they came home. She went on to tell Hannah about how she was approached and everything that happened afterwards. By the time that she was done, you would have thought that Hannah was a proud parent and Andrea had just received an award for the principal's list.

"You fell in love with that dick too, didn't you? I can see it all over your face," Hannah said after Andrea was finally done giving her the complete run down.

"What makes you think that?" Drea quizzed.

"Honey, it's all over your face. And shit, I can't say that I blame you by the story you just gave me," Hannah confessed.

"But, it was one night, right? You said do a one night thing and that's what I did. I'm not supposed to be stuck on that sexy ass man," Drea sighed.

"Hey, I don't make all the rules. I just break them a time or two. We can do you a for the dick challenge now girl… Drea flew to New York for some dick…had a one night stand for the dick… got sloppy drunk for the dick, and done fell in love wit the dick, aayyyeee…," Hannah laughed.

"Hannah, I'm gonna kick your ass," Andrea said, but she couldn't help but to laugh a little.

"But, for real though… if you wanna reach out to that man, do so. You have all of the resources to find anybody you want to, it's just one click away," Hannah told her.

"Nah… Ima just leave well enough alone. It was fun, it was good, but he can't be the man for me," Andrea tried to convince herself.

Chapter 13

The line for *Pressed* was wrapped around the corner. Lexi was never the type of person to go crazy over a celebrity, but she didn't knock those who did. Rasheeda was cool and all, but her clothes were too pricey and not worth waiting in that long ass line. Lexi only needed a few things from the mall anyway, thank God for that because she hated shopping there. She preferred going online, but didn't have time to wait for shipping, when all she needed was small items. She hit up the Nike store, where she grabbed a pair of black and gray leggings, with the hoodie to match. She then picked up a pair of all-black Air Max's 95, along with a pair of gray and purple ones. After she checked out there, some form of an unknown spirit pushed her into the Gucci store where she snatched up a purse and a pair of shades. Spending two-thousand dollars more than expected, she grabbed a soda from one of the small stands in the middle of the mall, then headed to her car. When she hopped in, her phone rang and the biggest smile crept across her face when a FaceTime from J.R. attempted to connect. Lexi quickly pulled down the sun visor and checked her reflection before sliding the bar across, answering the phone.

"You gon sit there and grin or you gon say what up?" J.R. said, licking his lips.

"You called me, you supposed to say sum," Lexi replied, slightly blushing.

"Mannnnnnnn...... you so fuckin pretty. Where you at?" he asked, brushing off her comment.

"I'm leaving the mall, where you at?"

"I'm around baby, I'm around," was all he said before placing a blunt to his lips.

It was something about that man that drove Lexi up a wall. She wasn't sure if it was his looks, the way he dressed, or his calm ass demeanor. He was so intriguing and nothing like the other dudes she fucked with.

"Where is around J.R."? she finally asked.

"I'm at my cousin's crib. Why? You finna slide through?" he asked, parting his mouth just a little bit, allowing the smoke from the blunt to release in the air.

"I can, I guess!"

"Aight, I'm about to text you the address, call me when you outside," he demanded before ending the FaceTime call.

Lexi contemplated whether or not she should run home real fast and change her clothes, but she knew with traffic on 285, she might fuck around and miss her beat, so she put some Carmex on her lips, took her curly weave out of the ponytail and headed to the address that J.R. sent.

It took her about an hour to get from Atlanta to Duluth, but the sweet sounds of Destiny Child's first album, *Writings on the Wall* distracted her from the antagonizing traffic. She sang along, impersonating all four members of the group before pulling into a nice housing complex. Lexi cut the music down before grabbing her phone, calling J.R., letting him know she had finally arrived. Within about two minutes, he came walking down the steps and over in her direction. He wore a pair of light blue jeans that fit his slim frame just perfect. A white Gucci collar shirt that housed a gold chain, with a Jesus piece attached. On his right wrist set a Rolex, while a gold Cuban-Link bracelet chilled on his left side. He had on a fresh pair of loose-laced Timbs and a crispy lining that peeked from underneath his Gucci skully.

Lexi unlocked the doors to her Benz right before J.R. reached for the door handle.

"What up, shorty!" J.R. smiled, closing her car door.

"Hello sir!" Lexi smiled back.

"This you right here? This motherfucker nice." he said, rubbing his hands across the dashboard of her car.

"Yeah, this me and thank you," she replied, looking away.

"You wanna come in? You ain't gotta sit in the car. My cousin just came home and it's a few of the homies in there and they ladies." J.R. informed her.

"Yeah, I'll come in for a little while," she agreed, getting out of the car.

Lexi headed towards the house while J.R. walked a few steps behind her, "Aye, give me a hug man." J.R. said, reaching forward, grabbing the tail end of Lexi's jean jacket, pulling her a few steps back.

Lexi didn't resist, she turned around and allowed J.R.'s arms to swallow her up. His scent hit her nose, making her knees weak. It felt so good being this close to him, after talking for a month, this was the closest she had gotten to him. After their embrace was over, J.R. took her inside the two-story home.

As soon as she walked inside, her vision was clouded by all the smoke that was lingering in the air. The house was beautiful, the living room was decorated with all off-white furniture and fixtures. It was about seven dudes in the room, most of them glued to the 72-inich television that hung on the wall. There was an intense game of 2K18 going on, the chicks in the room were either off in the corner on their phones or over the shoulder of their men, being their personal cheerleader.

"You want something to drink?" J.R. whispered in Lexi's ear.

"Nah, I'm straight," she replied.

"Cool… Come here and let me talk to you for a second," he said, grabbing her hand, pulling her into the huge kitchen.

Once inside, J.R. sat on one of the bar stools, he then pulled Lexi closer, where she was forced to stand between the gap in his legs.

"So, Miss Lexi, what's to you?" he asked, staring her in the eyes.

"Well, nothing much. I'm working, I'm in my last year at Clark… I mean, all this shit, I've told you before," she responded, looking away.

J.R. grabbed her by the chin, pulling her face back to his, "Always look a man in the eyes when they talking to you, but yeah, I know all that and that's the basic, I wanna know what's really to you." J.R. explained.

Lexi was at a loss for words, not that she was nervous, but she didn't know how to answer that question. Maybe she was slightly intimidated by him, but she would never admit that aloud.

"Honestly, I can read you a script right now, but it don't mean it's the truth. Knowing what's *"to me"* is getting to know me, being around me," Lexi replied.

J.R. smiled, laughing a little before saying, "How long it took you to think of that?"

"Boy shut up, that was from the heart," Lexi laughed, playfully punching him.

"Nah, straight up though, on some real shit. I wouldn't mind getting to know you, but I gotta be up front, I'm not that average nigga you probably used to fucking with. I can't sit on the phone and talk to you twenty-four seven, it's a lot of corny shit that I can't do…"

"Why it gotta be considered corny though?" she asked, cutting him off.

"You right, my bad. It's not necessarily corny, it's just the shit women like, I can't be on call all the time."

"And why not?" she quizzed.

"Cause I'm not that type of nigga, baby. I'm trying to build something, I need an empire and I need a lady who understands that."

"So, you are looking for a relationship?" Lexi asked.

"To be honest, not really, but if I met a shorty that makes me reconsider, then so be it." He hunched his shoulders.

Just as Lexi was about to reply, the sound of glass breaking caused the both of them to turn their heads.

"Nigga, you drunk as fuck, what the fuck you doing?" J.R. snapped, standing to his feet.

"My bad J.R. I did just fuck up, I ain't even try to do this." the boy said, finally looking up at the two of them.

"Aw shit J.R.... how you know this bitch?" the boy said, pointing to Lexi.

"Who the fuck is he calling a bitch?" Lexi snapped, walking towards him.

"Chill baby," J.R. turned around and said to Lexi before redirecting his attention back to that disrespectful clown.

"I'm calling you a bitch. You that lil hoe that dance at Blue Flame, I almost didn't recognize you with your clothes on," the dude said, bending over laughing at his own joke.

J.R.'s face instantly screwed up, he looked back at Lexi, then the unknown guy.

"Tez, nigga chill." J.R. said, addressing him first, then Lexi.

"You a stripper, ma?" he asked with a straight face.

"Bitch, I dare you to lie," Tez spoke up again.

"I said chill, homie." J.R. checked him, raising his voice just a little.

"Now, Lexi, I asked you a question. Do you strip?"

Lexi sat there for a moment, not believing her luck and how shit was unfolding right before her eyes. She had no choice but to tell him the truth since she technically was put on blast. She was afraid that admitting the truth, would cause J.R. to look at her differently, but she was left with no choice.

"Yeah, I dance at Blue Flame," she finally admitted, hanging her head low.

“What I just tell you a few minutes ago about looking a man in the eyes?” J.R. said, lifting up her chin once again.

“I told you that bitch a hoe.” Tez said, laughing even harder this time.

“Bitch nigga, didn’t I just say, SHUT THE FUCK UP!” J.R. roared as he held the gun he had swiftly removed from his waist to Tez’s head.

“My-my-my bad, J.R. I didn’t know….”

“YOU DIDN’T KNOW WHAT MOTHERFUCKER?” J.R. said, cutting him off.

Lexi stood off to the side with the other speculators who had joined them in the kitchen when they heard all the commotion.

“Mannnn cuz, come on, put ya strap away. That nigga don’t know no better.” J.R.’s cousin Reese spoke up, placing his hand on J.R.’s shoulder.

“This yo homie, I never liked this nigga anyway, so he is giving me a reason to blow his motherfucking brains out,” J.R. replied, placing his gun back in his waist.

The entire kitchen stood there in silence, afraid of what was going to happen next.

“Come on,” J.R. continued, grabbing Lexi yet again, pulling her outside this time.

Once they were on the porch, awkward silence fell upon them.

“I’m sorry about all that in there. Had I known some shit like that would have popped off, I wouldn’t have brought you around. I'll never put you in a fucked-up situation," J.R. apologized.

"It's cool, neither one of us knew that was going to happen." Lexi said, trying to down play the situation the best she could.

"Listen, I don't give a fuck about what you do to make your coins. I grew up around niggaz who robbed and killed for money, so I'll never frown my nose upon a woman who entertained people for hers. Imma be one hunnid with you though, if you and I start vibing and shit got serious, you might have to take another route, but we will cross that bridge when we get there. In the meantime, I'll be there to pick you up at nine for our date," J.R. said, kissing Lexi on the forehead, sending her on her way.

Chapter 14

The last couple of days that Alyssa had spent with Corey were nothing but pure bliss. Besides separating for work, she spent most of her time at Corey's Condo where they lounged around the house, ate, and made love. Since they discussed her doubt of being a good wife, Alyssa was thinking with a clear head and couldn't wait until the day she said "I do" to the man she loved. Alyssa was beaming from the inside out and she was even looking forward to going home the following week.

It was Friday afternoon and Alyssa didn't know what to do with herself. She was off for the weekend and with Corey working out of town, Alyssa had no plans. Tired of channel surfing, Alyssa grabbed her phone and FaceTimed her bestie. Seconds later, Kelly's face appeared on her screen.

"My A one since day one. Wassup boo?"

"I'm bored out of my mind, girl. I need something to do."

"Where's Corey?" Kelly inquired.

"Working out of town at a basketball game. You got anything planned for the night?" Alyssa responded.

"I had a date tonight, but I canceled that shit. One of my co-workers tried to set me up on a blind date and I found out that my date was a lame. I'm too fly to be seen with a sucka, Alyssa," she flipped her hair out of her face.

"I hear that," Alyssa chuckled.

"So, what are we doing tonight?" she continued.

"We can go to a club. I need to dance some of this stress away. It's been a long week and today ain't no better," Kelly vented.

"Okay. Grab some clothes when you get off work and come to my house. You take forever to get ready and I would like to make it to the club before one in the morning, Kels."

"Bitch, the club don't start popping until one in the morning, but to make you happy, I will be at your house by seven," Kelly rolled her eyes.

"Thank you. See you later," Alyssa bubbled.

"Later," Kelly replied and hung up.

Alyssa tossed her phone on the bed and walked over to the closet to start looking for an outfit for the night. She pulled out dresses, pants and tops and laid them on her bed. She tried on the clothes to see what outfit looked best and chose the best three outfits that she wanted Kelly to help her choose between. As she put the rest of her clothes back in the closet, she realized that she needed to go shopping before she went back home to Mississippi.

As the hours passed, Alyssa decided to tidy up the Condo to keep herself busy. When she was finished cleaning, it was a little after six. So, she decided to prepare a few pre-game snacks and drinks to hold them over until they got to the club. Around seven, the doorbell rung and Alyssa rushed over to answer the door knowing it was Kelly. They greeted each other with a hug before Kelly entered the house and the smell of food instantly hit her nose.

"Damn, A. You got it smelling good up in here!" She followed Alyssa to the kitchen.

"I figured we'd have a pre-game turn up before we hit the club. I made meatballs, wing dings, buffalo chicken dip with chips, and rolls for the meatballs. Do you want me to fix some margaritas or do you want to take shots?"

"I need shots and margaritas." Kels took a seat at the counter. "I'm trying to get loose."

"Well let's get started."

Alyssa grabbed the shot glasses from the cabinet and filled the glasses with peach Ciroc. They tossed the drinks back, poured some more and downed those as well. Kelly connected her phone to the bluetooth speaker in the living room and *Rake It Up* by Yo Gotti featuring Nikki Minaj came on. They twerked to the song as Alyssa made margaritas and Kelly filled her plate with food. When Nikki's verse started, they rapped it together.

"Brought out the pink Lamborghini just to race with Chyna, brought the race to China, just to race in China. Lil' bad Trini bitch but she mixed with China. Real thick vagina. Smuggle bricks to China...."

When the verse was over, they sat down, ate, and made small talk. After they were full on food and alcohol, they each went into one of the two bathrooms in the condo and got ready for the night.

Kelly was dressed in a strapless red bodycon dress with a pair of gold spiked Red Bottom pumps with matching gold accessories. Kelly chose the fitted light purple halter dress with silver Giuseppe pumps with diamond hoops and matching tennis bracelet. Alyssa's long weave had loose curls and Kelly wore her hair bone straight. The ladies took a few mirror pics together and a few selfies. Alyssa sent a few pictures to Corey before she uploaded them on social media. Instead of texting back,

Corey called to warn her not to forget who she belonged to, which was something he didn't have to remind her. After the brief phone call, the ladies took one more shot, grabbed their clutch bags, and headed out the door.

They arrived at club called Katra that was located on the Lower Eastside of New York around midnight. The line to get in the club was quite long, but when Kelly made her way to the front of the line, Alyssa knew her girl had things under control. She gave the bouncer their names and after he checked, he moved to the side to let them through. They walked inside like they owned the place and took a seat at the bar. They bobbed their head to the music and observed the crowd. That was Alyssa's first time there, so she didn't know much about it, but the club was nice and not over crowded, but the VIP section was packed.

After a few moments of sitting at the bar, it wasn't long before they got asked to dance and they accepted. They stood a few feet away from each other on the dance floor and turned up. The DJ played all the latest music and Alyssa was in her zone, but every time her dance partner tried to touch her waist or ass, she moved his hands. She danced for a few songs and told Kelly she was going to the bar before she left the floor. When she reached the bar, she ordered vodka and cranberry juice. As she waited for her drink, she looked around the club and spotted a man that looked like her target. She thought she was mistaken, but when she over heard someone say his name, it was confirmed that the man she was looking at was D'Mani. Alyssa pulled out her phone and tried to take a picture, but failed. He wouldn't keep still and there was always someone blocking her view, but that didn't stop her from keeping an eye on him throughout the night.

Alyssa and Kelly decided to leave the club at 3:30 in the morning. The club closed at four and they didn't want to get caught up in the let-out rush. D'Mani had left the club an hour before and Alyssa wanted to follow him, but she couldn't leave her friend behind. They walked a short distance to the car and Alyssa took her place behind the wheel since Kelly drove to the club. It wasn't long before Kelly was passed out in the passenger seat, which was something she always did after a night of partying. It had been that way since they were in college.

When they reached her Condo, Alyssa helped her bestie inside and took her to the extra bedroom and put her in bed. She walked down the hall to her room, got undressed, and put on a pair of tights with a tank top. Alyssa emptied out her clutch bag and grabbed her phone to let Corey know she made it home safely and that she loved him. Seconds later, he replied "I love you too and good night." She placed her phone on the nightstand, got comfortable, and laid there pissed off that she couldn't get a good picture of her mark before she drifted off to sleep.

Chapter 15

"Girl, did you hear anything I just said?" Lizz asked, tapping Anastasia's shoulder.

"Yeah, I did. You were talking about Harold's old pasty ass," Anastasia lied with ease.

All Lizz ever talked about was her husband, his money, and her side piece. She didn't work, unless you counted shopping as a job, and pretty much all she did with her days was fuck on her side nigga, and spend money all day. She was the true definition of a trophy wife, and while Anastasia loved her to death, she couldn't see herself being like her at all.

"Oh okay. Well anyway, he wanted me to suck on his little limp ass dick before I came here! Ain't nothin' attractive about a soggy noodle, girl! That shit look like fettuccini without the sauce!" Lizz carried on, making Anastasia almost spit out the smoothie she was sipping. She hadn't been listening before, but she was most definitely all ears then.

"Oh my God, girl you're a mess!" she laughed, shaking her head at her friend.

Honestly, she was glad for the humor because she had a lot on her mind. Of course, D'Mani was once again in his feelings about her leaving to go run to Richard, so he was ignoring her again. It was really starting to piss her off because it seemed like he didn't understand his position in her life. Sure, she cared about him, hell, she could even admit that she loved him, but that wouldn't change the fact that she was married and his income wasn't ideal or guaranteed. He acted as if she was supposed to be with him all day every day when really all she needed was some loving on the weekend like SZA. She rolled her eyes at the thought, but continued to pretend she was listening to Lizz as they walked through Fulton Mall with shopping bags on their arms.

"I swear I don't know how he thinks that his little ass shriveled up dick could satisfy me!" Lizz grumbled bitterly while shaking her head.

"I'm so glad I got bae ass cause if not, I would be deprived as hell!" she continued.

"Shit, who you tellin'? Richard ass be so damn predictable in bed that I got the shit down to a science. I know exactly what he's gonna do and when!" Anastasia bragged. "Not that he really does anything besides talk dirty," she rolled her eyes thinking of how lame the sex was with her husband, but she knew that with all of the perks would come some setbacks; she just wasn't expecting him to be so lousy in bed.

"He can't be THAT bad!" Lizz looked at her in disbelief.

"Naw, it's worse!" Anastasia watched as her brows furrowed and she tooted her lips like she was lying.

"Richard looks too good for his sex to be as bad as you're making it out to be," she rolled her eyes dismissing what she'd said.

Anastasia couldn't help but frown at her for saying something like that. She might not have cared too much for Richard, but she wasn't about to let Lizz talk about what his sex looked like. Noticing the change in her demeanor she immediately backtracked.

"I mean not like that… but, you know your man is fine," Lizz laughed nervously.

"Yeah, well you stick to your man and his struggling ass dick and leave mine alone," Anastasia said sharply instantly putting a stop to her laughter. Knowing that she wasn't about that fighting life from previous conversations, Lizz nodded and changed the subject.

"Okay…. let's go in here." She grabbed ahold of Anastasia's hand and led her into the Macy's they were passing.

Anastasia let out an irritated sigh, but allowed herself to be pulled inside of the store. Lizz tried to spark up a conversation as they browsed the clothes, but she was now in a bitter mood and really didn't want to hear shit else she was saying. No matter what anyone may think of her, she felt extremely territorial over Richard. He was still her husband and she wasn't trying to hear another female comment on his sex even if she was fucking someone else. Without saying anything to her Anastasia moved away to look at some other clothes while she still talked behind her. She picked up a couple of nice things she figured she could wear since she'd decided to go home for the holidays. Anastasia could only imagine how the shit was going to go with Andrea's stuck up ass, and Alexis' old ass kissing self. The only ally she felt like she would have, was Alyssa and she was acting real funny lately. If she was being honest with herself she would admit that the last thing she wanted to do was go home and be around her family in lame ass Mississippi. Still she figured since it had been so long since she had been home, it was time to show her face. Anastasia planned to do that and more looking good with her husband on her arm.

Satisfied with what she had, Anastasia made her way to the register, so that she could buy her items and go home. Seeing her getting ready to get checked out, Lizz walked over with her arms full and again tried to talk to Anastasia.

"Dang girl it looks like we both racked up!" she exclaimed giggling like Anastasia wasn't still pissed at her.

"Mmm Hmm," was all Anastasia felt the need to say. She quickly flitted her eyes from Lizz and to the sales lady.

"Look Ana. I'm sorry if what I said offended you, boo. I was just talking girl; you know I didn't mean anything," she apologized, but that shit didn't make any difference to Anastasia.

The deed was already done and she needed a break from Lizz, at least for the rest of the day. Wanting to shut her up Anastasia merely nodded, then stepped closer to the counter to set her things on top, hoping that Lizz would get the point.

Thankfully she did and she kept her mouth closed while the lady rang Anastasia up. The total came out to almost $2000 and she didn't even bat an eyelash as she handed over Richard's black card.

She gathered her things and moved to the side so that Lizz could get rung up. Of course, she tried to start a dry ass conversation up with the lady with her talkative ass. After Lizz got her total she reached into her olive Hermes bag and handed over her bae's card smiling hard as hell. The sales lady looked at the card for a second, then her eyes met Anastasia's briefly before she swiped it.

Not thinking anything of it, Anastasia checked her phone for a missed call or message from D'Mani even though she knew that there was none. She decided to send him another text, then stuffed her phone down into the pocket of her red pea coat. She knew it would go unanswered, but figured it was worth a shot.

"Come on girl, you ready?" Lizz flitted over to her and asked.

"Yeah, let's go. I'm ready to lay down before this fundraiser at Kyler's school," Anastasia sighed, leading the way out of the store.

"Me too. I don't know how shopping always makes me so tired," she laughed again further irritating Anastasia.

It seemed like she was nervous about something, and it was making Anastasia want to get away from her. They walked through the mall in silence until they made it outside to their parked cars. Anastasia popped her trunk and hurried to put her things away, damn near throwing them inside and slamming it closed. She shouted a good bye and got into her car pulling off before, Lizz could say anything else to her.

When she got home she was glad to see that Richard wasn't there. After dealing with Lizz's stupid ass, she couldn't handle a conversation with him, too. Letting out a sigh of relief she shut her car off and strutted around to get her bags out of the trunk. With her arms full of bags, she headed inside and up the stairs to their bedroom. Dropping everything at the door she climbed into the huge California king size bed in the middle of the room and passed out.

"Ana! Wake up! Why would you leave all of these bags in the doorway like this?" she woke up to Richard yelling and instantly wanted to go back to sleep.

"Because Rich, I'm tired!" she whined without making a move to get out of the bed or open her eyes. Even behind her closed lids she could tell that he was standing over her looking down in disapproval. Besides the many other things that she didn't like about Richard him whining about clutter was one of the biggest.

"How tired could you be from shopping? It would have only taken you like fifteen minutes to put all of this stuff away!" he shrilled and from the way that he was huffing and puffing she knew that he had taken it upon himself to put the clothes in the closet.

"Baby… just come lay down with me," she suggested not wanting to argue with him.

"Ana, it's twelve in the afternoon, it's much too early to be laying down," he dismissed causing her to finally open her lids to take him in.

He was dressed in some damn dad jeans and a Polo sweater. She watched him walk swiftly in and out of the closet and rolled her eyes at him. He was fussing under his breath as he started hanging up her things. Sometimes Anastasia wondered if the reason why he had female tendencies was because his ass was undercover. That would definitely explain why the sex was so dull.

"I can do that later Richard damn!" she snapped and climbed out of bed. He had managed to come in and ruin her nap with this mess and he knew she didn't play about her sleep no matter what time of day it was.

"I'm already doing it now, Anastasia! You know how I feel about clutter and you still left your stuff all over! Cleanliness is next to Godliness and we should all be aspiring to be more like him."

Anastasia already knew he was about to say that and she mouthed it with him in mockery. He was acting like a little bitch over some damn clothes that were in bags. It wasn't like she'd just left them all over the floor. She stood just inside of the closet door watching as he put all of her items onto hangers and hung them up.

"Ana, don't mock me! I can already tell that's what you're doing," he told her sternly. "I swear sometimes I wonder how your Mama raised you." Without even thinking Anastasia stepped fully into the closet and slapped him so hard her hand stung.

"Don't you ever talk about my mother, Richard! I let you walk around and say rude shit all the time, but my family is where I draw the line!" she shouted angrily. She could see that he instantly regretted what he'd said as he closed his eyes and sighed deeply.

"I didn't mean that, Ana…. I'm sorry," he apologized looking at her with sad eyes, but he could honestly save that shit as far as she was concerned. No matter what they had argued about she had never disrespected his mother and there were plenty of things she could have said about her baldheaded ass.

"I don't even want to hear that shit! You knew exactly what you were saying! You know what…… let me get the fuck outta here before I act a fool! And you better hope I don't tell my daddy what you said about his wife!" She left him there in the closet with a dumb ass look on his face, and snatched her purse up off of their night stand.

If she stayed around him any longer she was going to cut his ass and show him how deep the south really was in her. It was obvious that he let the fact that she had decorum fool him, but if he said anything else about her mama she was gone give him a cornbread, collard greens country ass whooping. She stomped down the stairs and out the door with him calling her name, but she didn't stop until she reached her car in the driveway. After taking a few deep breaths to calm herself down she pulled away wishing that she could go to D'Mani and never come back.

Chapter 16

It was Friday and Andrea had taken a work from home day so that she could take her mom to the doctor. She had a couple of hours before it was time to leave, so Andrea powered on her MacBook and started working on a case that was scheduled to go to court on the week after Thanksgiving. It seemed cut and dry when she took it, but as she dug deeper, she saw that the background of her client wasn't squeaky clean, so she was searching for loopholes. After an hour had passed, she hopped up and went and got in the shower. The hot water felt good on her skin, and she closed her eyes and her thoughts went right back to New York. Andrea had been battling with listening to Hannah and looking up the mystery man or just leaving it alone. Not wanting to seem desperate, she always stopped herself every time she was getting ready to search.

After washing off a few times, Andrea grabbed her plush towel and dried off. She had spent more time in the shower than she anticipated, so she picked up her pace because she knew that her mom didn't want to go to the doctor anyway, and it was up to her to be on time. Drea pulled a pair of black leather tights out of the third drawer and threw them on. She searched through her huge walk-in closet and pulled a red affliction on a hanger, put it on, then put on her black Uggs. The weather was in the fifties, and that was Ugg weather in Mississippi, so she took advantage of it on a day that she wasn't at the office.

Andrea called her mom right before she walked out and told her to head on outside. She heard her mom grunting, but she laughed it off. Her mom had been getting tired a lot lately and she had a constant cough, so Andrea made her an appointment with her primary care physician so that she could get a full check-up. Andrea thought that it was mostly men that didn't like to go to the doctor, but she was starting to see that it was older people in general. They felt like home remedies would fix everything. It was true that some worked, but Andrea felt like there was nothing wrong with going to the doctor either.

"I don't know why you forcing me to go to a doctor… I'm fine," Victoria said and coughed when she got into the car.

"That'll be determined shortly," Drea replied.

"Hmph," Victoria grunted.

"I'm getting dad to go to a check-up next, so don't think I'm beating up on you," Drea said.

"Good luck with that," Mrs. Holiday said.

Andrea pulled out of the driveway and made her way towards the clinic. She was taking her mom to see Dr. Kanisha Woodard Meaders. Andrea loved her humble spirit, and it was an added bonus that she was a black doctor. She knew that her mom would love her, so she cruised down the highway with her apple music on a gospel station just for mom. Twenty minutes later, they had arrived at their destination and Andrea was happy that she didn't have to hear the normal conversation about marriage and kids. As soon as the thought entered her mind, her mom made a comment.

"Look at that nice man over there. He would make a good husband," Victoria chirped.

"Mom, don't start," Drea rolled her eyes as she got out of the car.

"I'm just saying. You need to get married like Anastasia and set an example for your other little sisters. Anastasia listened and now she's married with a baby," Victoria continued.

The mention of her sisters made Andrea realize that she didn't even cuss the middle two out about standing her up in New York the week before. She made a mental note to text them in the group chat while they waited to be seen. They made their way inside and Andrea signed her mom in, then went and took a seat beside her. She pulled her phone out of her purse and clicked on the message icon. Andrea had to scroll down forever before she found the group chat labeled Holiday Sisters. It had been that long since they texted in the group and Drea shook her head. She hoped that thanksgiving would go well and they could somehow get closer. Honestly, they mostly used the chat to fuss, which was what Drea was about to do, but that didn't stop her.

Drea: It was real fucked up how y'all stood me up in New York! (rolling eyes emoji)

Stasia: Good morning to you too, rude ass.

Drea: Whatever! Why you didn't have the decency to tell me you weren't coming?

Lyssa: I was caught up at work… my bad Drea.

Drea: Where you work ay anyway, Lyssa?

Stasia: I got caught up Drea, but you forcing us to come home, so I'll see your ass next week.

Lexi: Yoooo y'all blowing me! I ain't got nothin to do wit this shit!!

Lexi: But heeyyyy Drea… hey Stasia and Lyssa!

Drea: Hey baby! I know you don't, but I just decided to text in the group because I was gonna make sure y'all haven't backed out from coming home next week.

Lexi: Yeah… I'm still coming.

Stasia: Yeah

Drea: I guess Alyssa has dipped out again… but anyways, they just called mom's name to see the doctor. See y'all next week.

Lexi: Wait, what's wrong with mommy?

Drea: Just a checkup. I'll call you later.

Andrea put her phone back in her purse and got up. It was clear that her mom wasn't going to get up until she did, so Drea led the way to the back. The nurse got Victoria's vitals, then asked the million and one questions that the nurse always asks, then they sat in the room waiting for the doctor to arrive.

"All this is for nothing… absolutely nothing," Victoria fussed.

"I'm cooking Thanksgiving dinner mom, and I'm gonna invite a few people over," Drea changed the subject.

"You know I'm gonna cook… I wish your sisters could come. They all too busy living their lives though," Victoria pouted.

"I'm gonna make it my business to get them here for Christmas," Drea assured her mom.

"Hello ladies… how's everything going today?" Dr. Meaders cheerfully spoke as she walked in with a big smile on her face.

"I'll be better when I'm back at home and outta this place," Victoria fussed.

"Aww don't be like that, Mrs. Holiday… we are going to get you checked out, and you'll be back home in no time," Dr. Meaders assured them.

It only took thirty minutes for the doctor to find out what the problem was. Victoria had an acute sinus infection. Andrea learned that her mom had been taking some over the counter medicines, but she needed a prescription to knock it out, so the doctor called her one in to the pharmacy. They left and decided to go and grocery shop for Thanksgiving before everything was picked over. Two hours later, they had all of the groceries they needed, Victoria's medicine, and headed back home. When Andrea parked, her phone began to ring. She pulled it out and instantly rolled her eyes when she saw who was calling.

"Answer it and invite him to Thanksgiving dinner. If you don't, I will," her mom said and Andrea noticed that her mom's eyes were glued to her phone.

Chapter 17

It had been a few days since J.R. took Lexi out on their first date, and although he told her that he wasn't the type of dude to be there for her every beck and call, he has been. They spent every day together for the past couple of days. They chilled at his crib, or caught up with each other in traffic, even if it was just for a hug or a quick meal. Lexi was really feeling J.R. and he had her full attention. She had this thing whereas, she only liked men for a short period of time before she lost interest, but it seemed as if, J.R. was doing new things every day to hold her attention. When he told her that he didn't judge people based off how they fed their families, he wasn't lying. The day he found out she was a stripper, she just knew that he would be turned off, but she was wrong. J.R. never bought up the fact that she stripped again and that was just fine by Lexi. Initially, she thought that he was some type of drug dealer, but the more she was around him, she knew things had to be deeper than that. J.R. had a lot of money and the way he was respected amongst his peers screamed POWER! She wanted to know exactly what type of business he was into, but she figured he'd share when the time was right.

Lexi sat in the middle of her bed, Indian style flipping through the channels when she decided to call her sister Drea. She hadn't really spoken to her since the day she TOLD her she was coming home. Lexi was giving her the silent treatment, but decided to end it when she got a Chase deposit in her bank account from Drea. She sent her $400.00 for the Jay-Z tickets she had purchased for Thanksgiving, as promised. Lexi was still pissed at the fact that she was missing out on seeing her favorite rapper perform, but chucked it up as a loss. She knew that wasn't going to be the last time the G.O.A.T had a concert, so she would just have to catch the next one.

Lexi Facetimed Drea and talked to her for a few minutes about Thanksgiving. It was Saturday and Lexi booked her flight to arrive Tuesday. Alyssa and Anastasia was coming in on Wednesday. Lexi wanted to spend some alone time with Drea before Pam and Gina arrived anyway. She was glad that she went ahead and made that call because talking to her sister actually had her looking forward to the holidays.

"You need me to take you to the airport Tuesday?" Bre walked in the room and asked.

"Nah, I'm good, J.R. said he was going to drop me off," Lexi replied, never looking in Bre's direction.

"Oh, aight!" Bre acknowledged before turning to leave.

Ever since the last time they got into it, Bre been real chill. Lexi forgot to curse her out about the threat that she made via text message, but in all honesty, she was tired of arguing with her. She knew that Bre wouldn't make good on her threat, so she wasn't really concerned. They walked throughout the house barely speaking to each other, which was fine by her. Lexi had Bre thinking that she was still going to New York for the concert. She knew that if Bre knew that she was going to Mississippi, she would invite herself over for dinner and since she'd been acting like ole girl off *Single White Female*, she continued to exclude that information.

Just as Lexi was about to get up and head to the kitchen to cook her something to eat, a message came in that made her smile.

J.R.: I gotta go out of town for a few days on business, I'm leaving tonight, but I gotta see you before I bounce. I'm finna slide thru right now since I'm over that way. I got yo fat ass some Chipotle. I'll be there in ten minutes.

Lexi: Ok. Thank you ☺

Lexi jumped out of the bed and ran to the bathroom to take a quick shower. She washed up twice before hopping out and drying off in record time. She threw on a pair of those new Nike leggings she got with a wife-beater. She snatched the bonnet off her head at the same time her phone chimed. J.R. sent a message telling her to open the door and she did. That was his first time he came in. He dropped Lexi off plenty of times before, but never came up, mainly because of Bre, but at that point she didn't give a fuck how Bre felt.

When Lexi opened up the door, J.R. was standing there with a brown bag from Chipotle and a large drink, all while holding his phone to his ear with the assistance of his shoulder. Lexi smiled at the sight of him before moving to the side, letting him in. J.R. sat the food on the coffee table in the living room before taking a seat.

"Aight nigga, let me call you back. I gotta holler at my girl about sum real quick," J.R. said to the person on the other end of the line before disconnecting the call.

Hearing him refer to Lexi as "his girl" caused chills to form all over her body. Although they never made anything official, she hoped and prayed that it was coming soon.

"What up, baby?" Lexi cheerfully greeted him, while flopping down on his lap.

"Shit! What's good beautiful?" he replied, grabbing her around the waist.

"Nothing, you tell me. What's with this business trip?" she inquired.

"Welllll, just know it's a business trip." He laughed before continuing, "And I gotta leave tonight to go to Louisiana, I won't be back til Saturday."

"Saturday? J.R., that's a whole week," she whined.

"Man, it ain't like you gone be in Atlanta anyway. Yo ass gon be in Mississippi until that Sunday," he stated.

Lexi had forgot about going home just that fast and since he had a point, she didn't complain.

"So, look, I just stopped by to see you before I bounce. I'm about to head out," he said before rising to his feet with her still on his lap.

Lexi stood to her feet, pouting, sticking her bottom lip out. J.R. looked at her before licking his lips, he then pulled her closer, grabbing her bottom lip with his lips, sucking on it briefly.

"When we both get back, we gon' do something special. I promise," J.R. said to her while grabbing as much of Lexi's ass, his hands could hold.

They shared a soft kiss before the sound of someone smacking their lips interrupted them.

"Oh, my bad," Lexi apologized, pulling away from J.R.

"J.R., this my best friend, Bre. Bre, this is J.R," she continued, introducing the two.

"Hey, how you, doin'?" J.R. spoke, giving off a slight head nod. Bre looked at the both of them before rolling her eyes and walking back into her room.

"Aight! Fuck you too then," J.R. shouted, loud enough for Bre to hear.

"I'm sorry about that," Lexi apologized for her best friend's rude behavior.

"Nah, its cool… Ya'll must be fucking though cause ma pressed," he stated walking towards the door.

"Ugh no!" was all Lexi could say as she walked behind him. She was glad his back was turned because she knew for a fact she had to be turning red.

"Well, she wanna fuck and you bet not be giving up none of my pussy," he replied, placing his hands between her legs.

"Your pussy? Last time I checked, we both was single," she said, smacking his hands away.

“Nah, I’m single, but you go with me., J.R. laughed and said before running down the stairs to his car.

Lexi stuck up her middle finger and closed the door. She grabbed her food off the table before heading to her room, she figured that she would get a few hours of studying in before she went to work that night. Her plans came to a halt when she opened up her bedroom door and found Bre laying in the middle of the bed, naked playing with herself.

“Damn, and now I need this bitch to take me to the airport,” Lexi mumbled before walking completely in the room and closing the door.

Chapter 18

Kelly and Alyssa spent the rest of their weekend chilling and watching movies. It had been months since they had a sleepover and Alyssa was more than happy to have the company. It was a hell of a lot better than sitting alone in the house, missing Corey. Alyssa enjoyed the weekend with her bestie and was a little upset when their weekend had to come to an end, but the upside to her weekend ending was that her man would be home the following morning and she couldn't wait to see him.

Alyssa spent most of her week at the FBI building discussing the next move in pursuing D'Mani. They had discussed the photos and the activity that went on at their locations and besides seeing him at club on Friday, only one of her team members had seen D'Mani and he wasn't doing anything incriminating. After a week and some change of staking out at their locations, none of her team members had gathered any useful evidence that they could us against D'Mani. To Alyssa, it seemed like they were wasting their time and that they should move on to another target, but their chief was confident that they would catch their target in the act eventually.

Before Alyssa left the FBI building on Wednesday, she informed the chief that she would be going home for the holidays and she would be there for a week or so. He told her to take all the time she needed with her folks and complimented her on a job well done which was a compliment she felt she didn't deserve, but accepted it anyway. As she walked out of the building, she sent a text to Anastasia letting her know that she was on her way to the restaurant and she replied that she was in route. They were meeting at Keens Steakhouse for lunch to catch up before they went home. Most of their time was going to be spent with the family and their spouses. So, they figured they'd meet up for some alone time.

Alyssa and Anastasia pulled up to the restaurant at the same time, which was about a half hour later. They parked their cars in the parking lot across the street from the restaurant. They hugged each other before they linked arms and walked into the restaurant to get out of the cold. Alyssa gave her name to the host and they were quickly escorted to their table. Alyssa made their reservation on Monday after her sister agreed to meet her. When they were seated, they buried their faces in the menus. A few minutes later, they placed their menus on the table. The vibe that Alyssa was getting from her sister wasn't a good one. Before she could speak, Anastasia did.

"Why are you staring at me, Alyssa?" she asked not looking up from her phone.

"Because I'm not liking this negative vibe I'm getting from you. Now, what's going on, Stasia?" Anastasia pushed her phone to the side and stared at her sister for a few seconds before responding.

"I like how you want to know what's going on with me, but don't want to inform me about what's going on in your life," she shot back catching Alyssa off guard.

Alyssa bit the inside of her jaw, which was something she did when she was nervous, scared, or trying to think of lie.

"And you better not fix your lips to lie to me, Alyssa. I will act a whole fool in this bitch if you do," Anastasia warned her.

"Okay. Fine. What do you want to know, Stasia?" Alyssa asked with her hands raised up.

"I want to know what's got you being so secretive that you can't even tell me about it. I knew why you didn't answer Drea back in the group chat, but this is me, Alyssa. We've always been tight and the fact that you're keeping shit from me is fucking with me for real."

"To be honest, I haven't told anybody about my new job, but when I tell you, you have to promise me that you won't judge me and you won't tell anyone. Not even your husband," Alyssa said.

"You know we're each other's walking diaries. Now, spill it." She leaned forward.

"I'm an FBI agent. That's why I had to quit working at your boutique." Anastasia burst into laughter and it instantly pissed Alyssa off. "What the fuck is so funny?" Alyssa fumed.

"Come on now, Lyssa. You? An FBI agent?" Her sister laughed some more.

Alyssa dug around in her purse for her badge and tossed it across the table to her sister. Anastasia picked up the wallet and stopped laughing when she saw that her sister was telling the truth. After admiring her badge for a few more seconds, she handed it back.

"Damn, sis. I'm sorry for laughing."

"If you reacted like that, imagine how the rest of the family is going to react. They probably won't believe it either." She folded her arms across her chest.

"What made you join the FBI?"

"I had to do something to keep up with y'all. You're an entrepreneur, wife, and mother. Drea is a successful lawyer and baby sis is in college trying to be great as well. I joined so I wouldn't be looked at as the failure of the family," Alyssa confessed.

Anastasia nodded her head in agreement. "Well, needless to say, I'm proud of you."

"Thanks sis," she smiled.

The waitress came over to take their food and drink orders. They ordered a Caesar salad and crab cakes for their appetizer and prime NY sirloin for their entrée. Anastasia ordered two bottles of White Wine before the waitress took off and Alyssa looked at her sister with a raised eye brow. Anastasia noticed the look on her sisters' face and held her hand up.

"Don't judge me, okay? I got a lot going on. Just be happy that I didn't buy the bar out."

"Damn! What the hell did Richard do now?" Alyssa quizzed.

"He's still the same asshole he's always been." She rolled her eyes. "But, that's not what's bothering me," Stasia continued.

"Then what is?" Alyssa asked.

"My side nigga is ignoring me and it's pissing me off." Alyssa's eyes widened at her sister's words, but she didn't speak. "I don't really feel like explaining the situation, but I will say this. Marriage is a life time commitment. If you're not one hundred percent about it, then take some time to think it through. There's nothing like loving two men at the same time," she shook her head.

Alyssa had plenty of questions running through her mind, but she didn't bother to ask. She figured that her sister was dealing with enough already and decided to leave it alone. She knew that Anastasia wasn't happy with her marriage, but she never expected her sister to have an affair. She figured her sister would just get a divorce, but that was easier said than done, she guessed. After hearing that her sister was having an affair, it made Alyssa question if she was really ready to marry Corey, but after seeing how her relationship was different from her sisters', she quickly pushed her doubts to the back of her head.

Minutes later, the waitress returned with their appetizers and two bottles of wine. After the waitress opened one of the bottles, she poured wine in each of their glasses before she disappeared. Anastasia downed her first glass and poured another one. Alyssa just shook her head and laughed at her sister. As they continued to talk, the subject of marriage went from negative to positive when Anastasia asked about her wedding plans. Alyssa showed her a few pictures of wedding dresses and her sister seemed to be very interested. She beamed as she talked about her wedding and she couldn't wait to discuss it with Corey.

Alyssa wasn't able to finish her food, but they finished both bottles of wine. She didn't realize she had drank that much until she went to pour some more and the bottle was empty. They had been talking about returning home in a few days and what was to be expected when they got there and that's when her drinking picked up. They talked about how their parents would probably take more interest in their careers and love lives than just them if they bothered to ask them questions at all. They both agreed to keep the drama to a minimum for their parents' sake, but they both knew that that was wishful thinking.

After Alyssa paid the bill, they walked to their cars and hugged each other good-bye. She was worried about Anastasia driving. Her sister felt like she drove better when she was drunk, but Alyssa didn't bother to argue with Anastasia's ridiculous statement. She jumped in her car and drove to the Boulevard Mall to shop for her trip back home. A couple of hours later, she walked out the mall with bags hanging from both her arms. She loaded the bags in the trunk, hopped in her car and drove home. Thoughts of Corey entered her mind and she was happy to see his car parked in front of her condo when she arrived home. Alyssa quickly hopped out of the car, grabbed her bags, and rushed inside to see her man.

When she got inside, she found Corey sitting on the couch. Dropping her bags, she straddled his lap and began to smoother his face with kisses, but when she didn't get a reaction out of him, she stopped.

"Baby, what's wrong? You not happy to see me?"

"What the fuck is this, Alyssa?" He held up a piece of paper in his right hand.

Alyssa glanced at the paper, she noticed that it was FBI welcome letter that she had placed in the drawer of her nightstand.

"Corey, what are you doing with that? You going through my shit now?

"I was lookin' for my watch that I placed in your nightstand drawer the last time I was here and when I went to get it, I found this. Now, answer my damn question." His anger began to show.

"I've been working as an FBI agent for the past month," she confessed.

"And you don't think that was somethin' you shoulda told me about? I thought you were still workin' at the boutique with ya sister. When the fuck was you goin' to tell me, you were the feds?" He slid Alyssa off his lap and stood up.

"Wait a minute? The fact that I'm a federal agent fucks with you?" She stood in front of him and placed her hands on her hip.

"The fact that you kept somethin' like this from me is what fucks with me the most. It's not like you left the boutique and started workin' for an ad company or some shit. You're a fuckin' federal agent and the fact that you kept this shit from me got me lookin' at you sideways now. Like you plottin' on me or some shit," he raised his voice.

"Corey, it's not like that. You know I wouldn't do no shit like that to you. I apologize for not telling you, bae, but this doesn't change shit, Corey."

"I don't know about that, Alyssa. I gotta think about this shit for a minute," he walked past her.

"Baby, wait," she pulled his arm.

"Are you still coming with me to Mississippi for Thanksgiving?"

"Naw. I'm a pass on that. I'm gonna spend the holidays with my folks." He snatched away from her.

"Corey, please don't be like that, nothing has changed about me. I'm still the same person!" She fought back her tears.

"I'll holla at you later, shawty," he stated in a harsh tone before he walked out the door.

The door slammed closed and Alyssa stood there frozen in place as her heart sank to her feet. She blamed herself for what had just happened and she was starting to regret not telling him sooner about her new career. She was aware of how Corey felt about law enforcement. He felt the same way most black people felt about the feds and cops, but despite his feelings, Alyssa wanted him to understand that she wasn't out to get him and that her being an agent was just her job.

Minutes after Corey left, Alyssa picked up her bags and carried them to her room where she began to pack. While she was packing, Kelly had FaceTimed her, but she didn't answer. She wasn't in the mood to talk. Her thoughts were wrapped up in Corey. The fact that she was going to be returning home alone upset her. Alyssa felt like being there with Corey would make her trip easier to deal with, but since he decided not to join her, she was dreading her trip home all over again.

Chapter 19

Ever since the rude ass comment that Richard had made about her mama, Anastasia had been giving him the silent treatment. How dare he come for her mama over something so trivial that she didn't have anything to do with. It took every ounce of home training she had not to go in on his cheap wig wearing ass mama. Fortunately for him, she just took the high road. After Anastasia left the house she went straight to Kyler's school and sat in the parking lot until it was time for her to go inside. Thank God for those little travel sized toothbrush things or else she would have had to pop a mint because she damn sure hadn't freshened up before leaving.

The hour Anastasia sat parked in the car gave her enough time to get her thoughts together because she was ready to say fuck everything and leave Richard for D'Mani for real. Just because he called himself mad didn't mean that he wouldn't welcome her with open arms if she decided to finally get a divorce. After about ten minutes of deep breathing exercises, Anastasia realized that leaving at that point would be stupid. She'd already sacrificed so much, and lost so many years and there was no way that she could let it all go for a thug that she could have very well met in Mississippi. Staying with Richard was only logical; he just had to know that she was not going to be treated with disrespect, and that included her family.

Once she came to terms with the decision to stay, she cleaned herself up, fixed her lipstick, and fluffed her hair. You would have never known that she'd been woken from a nap by her diva of a husband and had gotten ready in the car. There was nothing but compliments from the other parents and of course Kyler was spoken highly of. He did so well that she promised him a day of fun with just the two of them.

It was two days later, they were in the car in route to Madison Square Garden to see the Harlem Globetrotters. Her little man was a basketball fanatic and he loved everything that had to do with the game. It was definitely surprising to Anastasia since Richard didn't have an athletic bone in his body. Still she made it her business to keep him involved in basketball, by letting him go to the camps, watching every time a game came on TV, and everything in between.

Anastasia looked at her son in the rearview mirror and couldn't help the smile that came across her face. He was definitely the only highlight of that bullshit marriage, and her pride and joy. Most days she marveled at how handsome he was and couldn't believe that she'd carried him inside of her for nine months. He happened to be the same light complexion as her, with slanted eyes, and long thick eyelashes. They kept his hair cut short and he was starting to get waves since Anastasia insisted that he brush it every day. Originally, she had wanted to get his ear pierced, but Richard refused and acted like it would be the end of the world, so she let the fight go, but he was handsome without it.

"Ma, stop staring," he complained from the backseat and rolled his eyes causing her to chuckle and focus back on the rode briefly.

"Boy, I'm yo mama. I can stare at you all I want," she laughed at the frown he wore, glad that it didn't resemble the one that his father always seemed to have.

"Okay, okay, I'll leave you alone." She reached out to cut the radio up just as *Rake It Up* by Gotti came on.

Her eyes met her sons and they both began to sing and rap along bleeping out the curse words. Richard didn't like them listening to rap, he said that it was vulgar and violent, so when they were in the car with him they mostly listened to old school and R&B. Sometimes, Anastasia questioned whether or not Richard was really only twenty-eight with the way he acted. By the time the song was over, they were pulling into the venue and Kyler could barely control his excitement.

He bounced alongside his mother happily talking a mile a minute. His happiness was heartwarming to Anastasia and she couldn't help but feel the same way he did. After grabbing some snacks and drinks, they went out and enjoyed the show. Kyler even got a ball autographed by all the guys and learned a new dribbling trick. Anastasia had so much fun with Kyler that it was easy to forget the last week that had been full of drama, with Richard and D'Mani. She hadn't realized how stressful her life had been as of late until she got to spend some quality time with her son. Not even the short lunch she'd done with Alyssa had taken her mind off of everything like she thought it might. They'd discussed the trip home and Anastasia had been dreading it, but she knew that it was necessary. Kyler needed to be around family even though her sisters had yet to give him any cousins to play with, because all the kids in Richard's family was just as stuck up as he was. The tension in the house was really taking a toll on him, but today he seemed to enjoy himself and have fun like a normal kid.

After the show was over, Anastasia drove home listening to *PnB Rock* thinking of the upcoming trip. She'd planned on packing when they got home and she hoped that Richard wasn't throwing one of his bitch fits. After such a good day, all she wanted to do was grab a glass of wine and pack their bags for the trip. If she was being honest with herself, she could admit that she was fairly excited to see her parents and even her sisters. She hadn't been back to Mississippi in years, and although she talked a lot of shit, at that moment, she needed to be around some people who loved her because Richard was driving her crazy.

Anastasia looked back at Kyler and smiled as he slept, snoring loudly with his head thrown back and his arms wrapped tightly around his ball. She hadn't even realized how fast the trip home had been until she turned onto their block. Pulling into their driveway she was relieved to see that Richard wasn't there. Anastasia didn't have the energy to fight with him anymore and she knew that he would have something to say about something. She let out a relieved breath and shut off her car making sure to grab all of her things, so that she wouldn't have to come back out. She went around to grab Kyler and struggled a little bit under his weight and all of the other things she was carrying before catching her balance and strutting into the house. Surprisingly, he didn't make a sound as she carried him upstairs to his room and got him undressed and tucked in.

After she got him taken care of, she went down to the kitchen and poured herself a healthy glass of red wine. With her glass in one hand and the wine bottle in the other she made her way to their bedroom so that she could start packing. Flipping on the light as she entered, Anastasia took in the sight of their spotless bedroom and sat her items on the night stand before connecting her phone to the Bluetooth speaker. She turned to the Tony Braxton station on Pandora as she placed her suitcase on the bed and began to pack her clothes. It took longer than it should have because she had so many clothes, and since Richard had put her latest purchases away it took her awhile to find everything due to his "color coordinating".

She hummed along to each song as she sipped her wine and before she knew it, she was finished with packing and the bottle. Not wanting Richard to be able to come in and ruin her mood she lugged the now full suitcase off of her bed and dragged it back into the closet so that she could prepare for bed. Taking off her clothes she headed into the master bathroom and cut the shower on only waiting a few seconds before stepping under the hot relaxing spray. Her body tingled as she ran her loofa over her skin three times, then she rinsed off. After stepping out of the shower, she wrapped one of their plush white dry towels around her body before standing in front of the floor length mirror and looking at herself. She smiled at her reflection feeling a little conceited at the moment. Anastasia knew she looked too good to be with the likes of Richard and that she could have her pick of any man she wanted if she ever decided to part ways with him. She rolled her eyes at the thought since she wasn't going anywhere and went to the sink to brush her teeth for the night.

Once she was done cleaning her face and brushing her teeth she oiled her body and slipped on her panties and a pair of silk pajama bottoms and a white camisole. She could still feel her buzz as she cut off the light and slipped under the covers with the radio still playing in the background. The day had gone extremely well and it was even better since she didn't have to deal with Richard's nitpicking. She snuggled in the bed and closed her eyes as thoughts filled her head of seeing her family again after so many years.

When Monica's *Should Have Known Better* began to play and her mind drifted to the past. She didn't know if it was because she was drunk, or if the upcoming trip did it, but her mind drifted back to her childhood love, Zyree.

They had been together since her sophomore year in high school. His family had moved there from Chicago a year prior and he had still been struggling to figure out what everyone was saying when they talked. He sat down next to her in home room and asked her what the teacher was saying the entire period since her accent was so thick. They'd laughed together and played around instantly becoming friends. By the next year they were inseparable and Anastasia knew that she was in love. Her parents hated him because of his affiliation with Mississippi's biggest drug dealer, his uncle, Maine who'd he'd moved there with. Back then, she didn't share the same worries as them. Though there was no doubt about it Zyree was a thug, he still treated her with the upmost respect and never even pressured her about sex.

She planned on being with him no matter what her parents said and she would have if he had not gotten arrested around the time that she graduated high school. He'd managed to get caught with a few pounds of weed and had been carted off to jail only fueling her parent's fire. The 24 hours that he was held her parents scolded her for being involved with someone like him and told her how bad it looked on the family's part. Still, she wanted to be with him despite what they were saying until she found out the seriousness of his charges once he was released. He informed her of the amount of years he would have to do for such a crime and she began to feel as if maybe her parents were right. She didn't want to live a life of fear that he would be taken away from her. Though it was exciting and fun to be with him she wondered if she would be able to live the life of a drug dealer's wife. That's about the time that her father started to bring Richard around, and though she dated him to please them, she couldn't stay away from Zyree. She kept up appearances for the sake of her family, but she secretly continued to see him whenever she got the chance. Of course, he wasn't happy about the arrangement, but he understood and only wanted the best for her.

The night Richard proposed to her in front of her family, she felt pressured to say yes, but that night after everyone was in bed, she snuck away to see Zyree for one last time. When she no longer could hear the sounds of her parents moving around, Anastasia made her move. She jumped out of bed and slipped on a pair of jeans, and a sweat shirt and stuffed her feet into her sneakers trying to be as quiet as possible, so that she wouldn't wake Andrea. Just as she turned to open their window she heard Andrea clear her throat quietly.

"Ooh hoe you sneakin' out to see that thug ain't you?" Turning around, she met eyes with her sister who was sitting up on the side of the bed with a shit eating grin. Anastasia didn't have time to play games with her big sister.

"Please don't say nothin' Andrea, damn!" she hissed looking from her to the door scared that their conversation would wake their parents. Mrs. Holiday had bionic ears and could probably hear a mouse pissing on cotton, so the last thing she needed was to be caught because of Andrea's big mouth.

"Mama gone beat yo ass, girl! Didn't you just get engaged? How the hell you creepin' already?" she teased like it was a joke until Anastasia sneered in her direction. "Okay, okay, but if you want me to keep your secret I'm need something in return."

Tired of the back and forth Anastasia had to agree.

"Anything you want." Anastasia nodded.

"Anything?" Drea quizzed.

"Yes bitch! Anything! Now, can I go?"

Andrea smiled sneakily and gestured towards the window for her sister to go ahead. There was no telling what brown nosing Andrea would require of her to keep this secret, but right now, it was a matter of life and death. With her sister's approval, Anastasia climbed out of the open window and stretched her body, so that she could grab ahold of the tree next to it. She shimmied down and ran to Zyree's awaiting car and jumped inside quietly closing the door behind her. She leaned over and gave him a kiss before he pulled off into the night.

The ride was a quiet one as they both probably had a lot of things on their minds. Her with the impending wedding and him with his upcoming trial. When he finally pulled into the driveway of his apartment, he cut the car off and turned to her with those beautiful brown eyes.

"Come on, ma," he said leading the way inside.

Anastasia went over how she would break the news to him in her mind as she followed him in the house and to his room. No matter how she said it, she knew it would be a hard pill to swallow, so she elected to just blurt it out.

"They want me to marry Richard," she told him as they entered his room. He had still been in front of he,r so his back was turned, but he whipped around with a scowl as soon as the words left her mouth.

"That Buford ass nigga?" he asked, even though he knew exactly who she was talking about.

"Yeah... he proposed tonight... and you know how my parents are so... I had to say yes.... But, I swear we can run away! I don't want to marry him! If we leave, I won't have to!" she rambled trying to lighten the blow of her news.

He sat down on his bed and dropped his head into his hands before really looking at her for the first time since she'd gotten in the car. He looked at her ring and scoffed letting out a bitter laugh, then shook his head.

"Anastasia, you know I can't leave here. I'm being groomed to take over.... I gotta stay. Plus, where you gonna run anyway when a nigga bouta be sat down for at least 5 years?" He wanted to know.

She sat down beside him and sighed deeply because she hadn't thought of any of that when she'd come up with the idea to run. Tears filled her eyes at the thought of being taken away from him. She felt him put his arm around her shoulder before lifting her chin.

"I can't lie baby, I'm fucked up about this shit.... But, what kind of man would I be to make you wait for me? You got a whole life to live..."

"What are you sayin? You don't wanna be with me?" she cried, hurt that he was just letting her go without a fight.

"Hell naw! If I could, I'd run wherever you wanna go... I swear, but you deserve so much better than no contact visits and 30 minute calls. I don't want that for you ma and as fucked up as your parents are they're right about me being no good for you."

Anastasia couldn't understand why he was saying these things when all she wanted was him. There was no way she could live a happy life with Richard, when her heart was with Zyree. She tried to reason with him, but he wasn't budging from his decision. With no more points to argue, she elected to give him something that her parents or Richard couldn't take and that was her virginity. She had been waiting for a special time to tell him that she was ready, and she felt like now, as they were saying good bye, would be the best time. Anastasia showed Zyree her love with her body that night and he did the same, taking extra care to be gentle with her. She spent the entire night in his bed not thinking of her parents, or Richard, or her responsibility to make the family look good by marrying well.

Two months later, her and Richard were married with a baby on the way and Zyree was headed to serve his time in the department of corrections. She used to think about that night often, but as time wore on and she left Mississippi, Zyree became a distant memory.

Now, with the trip coming up he was back on her mind and she wondered if he'd gotten out yet. She went back and forth over what could have been had he allowed her to follow her heart and stick it out with him. Shaking her head, Anastasia turned over so that she could go to sleep. Things were how they should be and where ever Zyree was at that moment, she was more than positive that she was the last thing on his mind.

Chapter 20

"Heeyyy Lexi!" Drea sang right after she answered her baby sister's FaceTime call.

"Heeyyy biitttccchhhh!" Lexi sang back.

"When are you getting here? You know we gotta spend some time together without those other two before the holiday," Drea said as she slipped on her blue jean jacket and grabbed her car keys.

"I literally just booked my flight and was bout to text you… I get in Tuesday morning at ten… and you right, we gotta kick it before them bougie sisters get here. That's why I'm coming a day early," Lexi replied.

"Good… you inviting anybody to dinner?" Drea quizzed.

"Noooo… but, I'm bringing my new boo for Christmas. I'm working on it now," Lexi beamed.

"Oh lawd… we gotta catch up on everything Tuesday… you better get your mama though. I think she tryna invite Joseph and we gon have some problems," Drea fussed.

"That lame ass nigga knows not to show up even if she does," Lexi hissed.

"You would think, but he is a damn fool that has her fooled… Anyways, let me get outta here, so I can go meet Hannah and do some shopping," Drea told her sister.

They said their goodbyes and Andrea went and got in her car and crunk up. After sitting there for a few minutes, Andrea backed out and mad her way towards County Line Road where she was about to meet Hannah at North Park Mall. For the first time ever, Drea was behind on Christmas shopping. She normally did most of her shopping online, but going into the stores to catch random sales was always a must. Even though her sisters were distant and acted crazy as hell, she still brought them gifts. The only thing that she had bought so far was an iPad for her nephew, Kyler. Drea hoped to grab a few things for her parents, then maybe her sisters wouldn't mind getting up Friday and doing some Black Friday shopping. Cyber Monday was going to be so lit, Drea already knew.

Twenty minutes later, Andrea made it to the mall and drove around and parked at Belk where she always met her friend. Just when she parked, her phone rang and when it connected to the Bluetooth, Hannah's voice invaded the car.

"I'm pulling up now… I know yo precise ass was gonna be calling at any moment. I'm passing by Krispy Kreme right now," Hannah stated.

"I knew I was gonna beat yo slow ass anyway, so I didn't rush. I just parked. I'll wait for you," Drea laughed and hung up.

Andrea clicked on the Snapchat app and viewed a few stories while she waited on Hannah. She knew that if Hannah said that she was already on County Line Road, that meant that she was really still on Interstate 55. After laughing at a few videos, Andrea looked up and was shocked as hell to see Hannah's black Honda Accord pulling up beside her car and parking. She turned the car off, threw her phone in her purse, and got out.

"Yeeaahhh I know you thought my ass was lying, but nope. I told you I'm doing better," Hannah smirked after she parked and got out.

"I can't even lie… I just knew I was bout to be waiting at least ten more minutes," Drea laughed.

They made their way inside and Andrea went straight to the right where the shoes were. Shoes were a weakness of hers, which would explain why she had a whole walk-in closet filled with shoes only, that were still in the boxes. She could go straight to whatever pair she had in mind without second guessing. A pair of tan Steve Madden boots caught her eyes that would go perfect with the outfit that she had in mind for Thanksgiving. Andrea asked one of the sales women for her size, and she brought them back in less than five minutes. As soon as she put them on and stood up, Drea knew that was about to be her first purchase of the day.

Two hours and several bags later, the ladies were walking out of the mall with bags from Belk, Dillard's, H & M, JC Penny's, Rue 21, and Love Culture. Andrea bought her parents a few things, as well as her sisters and a few other family members. She was the one who was known for going above and beyond for everyone during the holidays.

"You wanna go to the M Bar tonight?" Hannah asked as they walked out.

"Hmmm… nah Ima pass on that. Maybe next week. I missed church last Sunday and daddy bout had a heart attack, so Ima go to bed early tonight, so I can make it tomorrow," Drea told her friend.

"Mr. Abraham still tryna hook you up with Deacon Andrews's son?" Hannah chuckled.

"Girl… yes," Drea rolled her eyes.

"Mommy too… they might as well stop though," Drea continued and Hannah couldn't stop laughing.

"I want you to find love too, but they gotta chill out," Hannah said.

"Call me crazy if you want, but I think it's gonna end up being Mr. New York," Hannah chattered.

"Girl stop ittt… you still on that. Just when I stopped thinking about him, you bring him up," Drea fussed.

"Bitch please, you ain't forgot about that man. You probably pull your vibrator out every night and get off reminiscing about that night," Hannah hinted.

Instead of replying, Andrea just flipped her the bird. She wasn't about to give her friend the satisfaction of being right. She would eventually confess, but she wasn't about to right then. At that very moment, Andrea made up in her mind that she was going to reach out to her mystery man after the holidays, she just hoped that she could hold out that long. That man had fucked her so good that she was feenin' for him.

"Find that man girl," Hannah teased her.

"Bye Hannah... Come to church tomorrow if you get up in time," Drea told her friend, then they parted ways.

On Tuesday morning, Andrea woke up and was still in a pissed off mood. She had turned her phone off Sunday after church, went and got a hotel room in Pearl, and shut the entire world out. Her parents had pissed her off so bad and she knew that if she stayed at home, they would only walk next door and further piss her off. Andrea got a room out that way because it was near the airport and she could easily pick Lexi up. She didn't even go into the office the day before, she worked straight from the room.

When it was thirty minutes until ten, Andrea finally checked out of the room that she had been occupying and headed towards the airport. She knew that Lexi was flying Delta because that's what they always flew, so she took her time getting to the airport, so that she could park right near the arriving flights. Of course, they never wanted anyone to park, but the airport wasn't big, so if anyone fussed, they were only being an asshole. Drea made it to the airport and pulled over and parked in the long-term parking lot just to let a little time pass by. She turned her phone on for the first time since Sunday, and text messages started pouring in. The only name she clicked on was her baby sister's, so that she could confirm that she was on the plane. She saw that text, and ignored the rest, along with all of the voicemails. Hannah had even called, but since she was at church, she already knew how pissed off she was, so she knew that her friend understood what she was dealing with.

At twenty minutes after ten, Andrea made her way towards the arriving flights section. Just like clockwork, she saw Lexi walking out of the doors just as she made it to the Delta terminal. Her sister was fly as hell dressed in a pair of ripped boyfriend jeans and a Gucci everything else. Andrea knew that the outfit on her sister, including the sunglasses had to cost at least two stacks. She popped the trunk, so that Lexi could put her bags in.

"Why the fuck you ain't been answering the phone?" Lexi snapped as soon as she got in.

"Trust me, Ima tell you as soon as we go eat and grab some drinks… but, you looking fly as hell baby sis. You got a sugar daddy over in the A?" Drea queried.

"Hell naw… ion want no old ass man," Lexi grimaced.

Andrea wanted to ask her where the hell she was getting money to buy such expensive clothes, but Lexi's phone chimed with a text and her attention went straight to the phone. She could tell that whoever her sister was talking to was very special judging by the smile that was plastered on her face. Instead of interrupting her sister, Andrea headed towards The Iron Horse Grill, so that they could eat and have a few drinks. It was only about elven o'clock in the morning, but it was five o'clock somewhere. About twenty minutes later, Drea parked on the side street to the restaurant and finally pulled Lexi from her phone.

"Lexxiiii… who got you skinning and grinning all in that phone? You would normally been done threw the shit in your bag by now," Drea coaxed.

"Dreeeaaaa… his name is J.R. and he is soooo dope. I really like him… but, I'm not sure if mommy and daddy will," Lexi whined.

"Hmph… don't let them pick a man for you," Drea mumbled and got out of the car.

"Damn why you walking so fast?" Lexi fussed behind her.

"Because I'm ready to get a drink, so bring ya ass on," Drea informed.

They walked in and were seated right away since it was so early. The waitress led them to a round table and before she could walk away, Andrea ordered a double shot of red berry Ciroc for her and a single for Lexi.

"Shiiidddd make mine a double, too," Lexi chimed in.

A few minutes later, their drinks were placed in front of them, and Andrea threw hers back in no time. Alexis wasted no time following suit. They ordered some wings and cheese sticks as an appetizer, and another round of drinks.

"Now, what's got you drinking so early in the morning? Not that I mind the free drinks… but, ya know," Lexi quizzed.

Drea rubbed her temples with both hands, sighed, and then prepared herself to tell her sister what the deal was. She was glad that she came home a day early because there was no way that she was going to vent in front of the others. Andrea reached into her purse and pulled out the princess cut diamond ring that had been given to her at church on Sunday.

"You getting married? To who bitch? Why you so salty about it?" Lexi fired questions back to back to back.

"After daddy finished preaching, out of the blue he called me up to the front. I didn't think anything of it because you know how he is, always bragging on us to the congregation and shit… but, when he said he was proud of the step that I was about to take and called Joseph up too, I wanted to choke his ass. I locked eyes with mom and I knew that she knew what was going on by the look on her face. So anyway, Joseph walked his happy ass up there, got down on one knee, grabbed my hand, and slipped the ring on without even asking me shit. The congregation erupted in applause and I was fuckin livid. As soon as service ended, I stormed out, went and got a room at the Marriott, and that's where I been since Sunday… with my phone turned completely off," Drea ran everything down to her sister.

"Wait a damn minute!! Do they not know about Joseph? The fuck? They be tripping too hard on this marrying us off shit," Lexi retorted.

"Lexi, I wanted to strangle both of them, but I just decided to steer clear of them. Now, I have to try to put all of this shit outta my mind and enjoy Thanksgiving since it's the first time that all of us will actually be together in years. It's gon be hard though," Drea admitted.

"It's gon be okay sis… you know I got ya back," Lexi expressed.

The two of them ate and drank for the next couple of hours. When they were done, they made a few more stops, and left the most important one for last, which was the liquor store. Lexi decided that she would stay with Andrea that night, and get up and surprise her parents the next morning. They were all planning to stay with their parents, just like old times. Andrea couldn't shake the nagging feeling that all hell was about to break loose.

Chapter 21

The day had finally arrived for them to board their plane heading to Mississippi and Anastasia was filled with mixed emotions. She wanted to see her family and gloat about all that she had going for herself, but at the same time she wasn't sure if Richard would be able to keep up the persona of a loving husband. He was already irritating her and they hadn't even left yet. She rolled her eyes into her head as he complained for the hundredth time about the delay with their flight.

"Rich, I wish you would calm down, and stop being so damn extra," she sighed with her eyes still closed. He was silent for a second, so she knew that he was looking at her with that sour face he always made when he was annoyed.

"No Anastasia, extra is our flight being delayed for over an hour, and having to sit in these uncomfortable ass chairs. That's extra! It's already 2 a.m.! We should have left by now," he grumbled and she knew he was upset because he had let a curse word slip.

"Well, I told you not to wear that Richard. You would have been much more comfortable had you dressed more casual," she told him holding in a laugh at his expense.

Most people taking a flight at this time of morning dressed in loose fitting comfortable clothing, but his ass refused and instead elected to wear his signature khakis and polo. Anastasia had worn a pair of PINK, black and gray leggings with leg warmers, the matching shirt and jacket and some dark gray UGGs. Kyler had on a maroon and dark blue sweat suit with blue and maroon new balances on his feet. He was so comfortable that he'd fallen asleep not too long after they arrived and was still knocked out with his head in Anastasia's lap.

"I never said I wasn't comfortable, and this is casual, Anastasia. You act like I'm wearing a suit or something," he argued defensively.

"You might as well be," Anastasia mumbled dryly.

"Now, is not the time for that smart mouth of yours, Ana. I am not in the mood right now," he went off on a tangent as usual and instead of arguing with him, Anastasia pulled out her headphones and tuned him out. She knew that he wouldn't want to cause a scene there at the airport, so he wouldn't raise his voice. Cutting up the volume as high as she could stand it, Anastasia ignored Richard hoping that he didn't act a fool the entire time they were on the plane, too.

She dozed off and Richard nudged her awake not too long after that to let her know that their flight was boarding. She gathered her things while he lifted Kyler up into his arms and they all trudged to their gate. He seemed to have calmed down as they took their seats in first class with her by the window and Kyler sitting next to her and Richard sitting in the seat ahead of them. They fastened themselves in and were right back out of it before the plane was in the air good. The four-hour flight went by fast as they slept and it seemed as if they had just sat down by the time that they were landing, the sound of the pilot awakened Anastasia. She looked out of the window at the sun rising over the clouds and dread invaded her body. It had been years since she'd been back and she just knew that there was bound to be tension and catfights with her and her sisters. Shaking off the feeling, she prepared herself for her and Kyler to exit the plane.

After getting their bags and renting a car, it was already a little after six and Richard was still in a pissy mood. Anastasia couldn't understand how he could be so irritable when he booked the flight at that time of the morning. He claimed it was more practical to travel at that time like they didn't have a five-year-old who would be tired. She was actually surprised that Kyler hadn't been too difficult due to his sleep being disrupted, but he was perfectly behaved. It was Richard being the brat. Anastasia and Kyler sat in the car while he finished the paperwork for it and soon he was getting in also. She ignored his grumbling about the time and the hassle of renting a car while they pulled away from the curb, headed to her parent's house. In an effort to keep the peace she didn't even complain like she normally would when he got in and turned the station to some off the wall ass light Rock. She didn't say anything, but she couldn't stop the side-eye she gave him. Richard acted like he took it up the ass, but for appearances sake she needed to hold things together, and she was doing good until he passed their exit.

"Rich, you missed the exit!" she said loudly thinking it was a simple mistake.

"I know that, Ana. I booked us a suite out in Brandon. I know you didn't think we would be staying with your parents?" He shrugged without taking his eyes off the road, like the decision had been obvious. "Besides, I have a conference out that way and Brandon is much closer than Madison."

Anastasia's mouth dropped open at what he'd just said. Not only had he not planned to have her a half hour away from her family, but he was going to be working also. She couldn't help but think that this was another reason why she couldn't be faithful in her marriage. Richard acted as if his job was his wife and she was the damn mistress. She stared at him in disbelief before she felt her face ball up in rage.

"Are you fuckin' shittin me? You know I haven't been home in years and not only do you want our family in a damn hotel, but you're gonna be busy with a conference, too! It's fuckin' Thanksgivings for Christ's sake! What could you possibly have to work on during the holidays?" She wanted to know all of her patience were worn thin at that point.

She had really been trying to be the bigger person during the trip, but Richard was determined to ruin that. Anastasia couldn't understand why he was always trying to be her father and not her damn husband. He never discussed things with her, he always just made plans, then told her about them like she shouldn't have a say in their lives. She watched as he took a deep breath and swallowed hard as if he was about to say something, but he just continued to drive like she hadn't asked him anything. Of course, he was probably pissed about her using profanity, but what did he expect? He was trying to keep her away from her family during the holidays. She was already a ball of nerves having to see them after so long, and now his ass probably wasn't going to be around to at least portray a strong front against her annoying ass sisters. When he still hadn't said anything, she turned completely in her seat to face him.

"Hello! I know you heard me!" Anastasia yelled.

"Keep your voice down," he grunted taking a glance in the rearview at Kyler, who was still sleeping.

"I will not! You know how important it is for me that we look the part, Richard! My sister's will all be there-."

"Anastasia, you don't even like your sisters, so why would it matter what they think about anything? You kill me being ghetto and bourgeois at the same time," he scoffed cutting her off. "Your sisters don't even like me and I don't like them either, so staying in a hotel was always the plan. As far as work goes, you know what I do and I never hear you complain when you're shopping or taking trips, so don't complain now, but if you're dead set on staying with your family, I will drop you and Kyler off, but I'm still going to the hotel," he rattled off.

"You know what… I don't even care, take me the fuck home then," she snapped angrily sitting back into her seat and folding her arms while he mumbled under his breath about her cursing.

She was in the mood to drop f-bombs on him the entire way to her parent's house, but she didn't even want to say that to him. They hadn't been in Mississippi a good three hours and he was already fucking up the entire trip. She just knew that Andrea and Alexis's messy asses would be the first to comment about him not being there. How do you show off accomplishments when the biggest part of it wasn't even around? She took a deep breath as they pulled onto their old block and gave herself a mental pep talk. If there was nothing else she could do, she could act her ass off and that's exactly what she planned on doing. She'd just explain that Richard had an important conference to get to and it was for a promotion. Throwing on a smile even though her heart was beating a mile a minute she stepped out of the car as soon as it came to a stop in front of her childhood home.

"Here goes nothing," she mumbled walking up onto the porch after grabbing her and Kyler's luggage.

Chapter 22

Andrea made margaritas for her and Lexi, and they sat up and drank and caught up with each other until about midnight. Victoria called, and Andrea finally answered because she didn't want any tension when everyone else arrived. She knew that she was going to have to have a good talk with her parents, but she hoped that they could at least make it through the holidays with no drama, so that they could enjoy having all of their kids at home at the same time. Andrea felt like that should trump everything, everyone being at home for a happy occasion and not a death.

Out of all of the talking that Lexi did, Drea still hadn't figured out where her baby sister was getting all of her money from. When she pulled her clothes out of her suitcase, everything still had tags and not one piece of clothing was cheap. She knew that their mom sent Lexi money, but she couldn't imagine it being enough to buy the shit that she had. Instead of saying anything, she sucked it up and headed off to bed because she needed to be up and at their parents by six the next morning to start preparing breakfast.

Andrea set her alarm for five thirty, said her prayers, then drifted off to sleep. When her alarm tone sounded, she felt like she had only been sleep for an hour, but she got up and was actually in a good mood and ready to see everyone. Drea took care of her hygiene, threw on a pair of tights, a Tougaloo sweatshirt, and red chucks, then went and peeked in on Lexi.

"Hey Lex, I'm going to start cooking. Go on and get up so mommy can see you and leave me alone," Drea told her.

"It's toooo early, bitch," Lexi grumbled.

"Girl, get yo ass up," Drea demanded and Lexi rolled over and fussed, but she got on up.

Andrea heard Lexi mumbling, but she paid her no mind as she grabbed her phone and a few more items and left. She knew that her little spoiled ass would be over there soon to see their mom since she was her favorite. Drea used her key to unlock the door when she made it to her parent's. It was only about fifty degrees, but the weather for the rest of the week and weekend was supposed to be in the seventies. Drea heard her mom in the kitchen as soon as she walked in.

"Good morning, mom," she spoke and the smell of coffee filled her nostrils.

"Good morning, Drea… you know you scared us half to death disappearing like that," Victoria told her.

"I had to leave to keep the peace, mom. Where's dad?" Drea asked.

"Hey sweetheart. I'm right here," he appeared in the doorway and spoke.

"Hi daddy," Drea spoke.

"I came over to cook breakfast," Drea announced.

"What's the occasion?" Victoria asked.

"Just family and love," Drea smiled and began pulling pots and pans out of the cabinets and food items from the pantry and refrigerator.

"You expecting someone? That's a lot of stuff you took out," her mom asked.

"You wanna help?" Drea changed the subject.

"I'll be in my study," Abraham told them and left them alone.

"Sure… what all are we cooking?" Victoria inquired.

"A sample of everything," Drea smiled as she poured flour in a bottle to prepare some homemade pancakes.

The aroma of food filled the house and forty minutes later, Drea heard the front door open and she knew that it had to be Lexi. Her mom was too busy checking the bacon in the oven to notice her baby girl come in.

"Mommyyyy!!" Lexi sang and ran up and hugged her.

"Lexi… baby! Oh my Lord… what are you… I'm so happy to see you. Girl, you skin and bones. Ima fix you two plates," Victoria bubbled as she hugged the baby of the family tight.

"I eat mommy… I just workout like three to four good times a week and it keeps me in shape," Lexi said.

"What kinda working out?" Drea mumbled and Lexi winked at her.

"What you say, Drea?" Victoria inquired.

"Nothing mom," Drea replied and a queasy feeling came over her.

Andrea rushed to the bathroom and barely made it to the toilet before the contents in her stomach came gushing out. The feeling came over Andrea so fast that she almost didn't have time to react.

"Bitch, you thirty and can't hold ya liquor?" Lexi said from the door.

"Shut the hell up," Drea said and flipped her sister off.

She heard Lexi laughing as she walked off and rolled her eyes. Andrea opened the cabinet and grabbed a towel and one of the new toothbrushes that they always kept a supply of and opened it. After she washed her face, she brushed her teeth and gargled with some Listerine. She had no idea what had just came over her, but whatever it was, it needed to leave because Andrea was ready to enjoy the holidays with her family. When Drea walked back to the front, she heard Lexi talking to their dad.

Before she made it back to the kitchen, the front door opened and she locked eyes with Anastasia.

"Hey Stasia… so glad y'all made it… heeyyy nephew!" Andrea said and hugged both of them.

"Hey Drea… I told you we were coming," Anastasia replied.

"Yeah just like you were meeting me for dinner a few weeks ago," Drea rolled her eyes.

"Whatever," Anastasia mumbled.

"Anastasia… Kyler! Oh, my goodness! Y'all come give me a hug," Victoria came out of the kitchen and said.

"Wait… is Richard leaving?" Andrea asked as she looked out the door at the back of a car leaving.

"Yeah, he gotta go take care of some stuff," Anastasia perked up and replied.

Andrea wanted to pry because the words that Anastasia had just spoke seemed rehearsed to her, but she dropped it for the time being. Anastasia went and spoke to their dad and Andrea went and grabbed her phone to text Alyssa to see how far away she was. She figured that she wouldn't reply, but it was still worth a try in her eyes.

Andrea: Good morning… how far away are you?

She sat her phone on the counter and started breaking eggs. Some to scramble with cheese and some to use for the French Toast batter. Five minutes had passed and Alyssa still hadn't replied, so Andrea texted her again.

Andrea: I figured you wouldn't reply, (rolling eyes emoji) but breakfast is almost ready.

"I'm so glad to have y'all here… I hope Alyssa is on the way," Victoria beamed when she walked back into the kitchen.

Thirty minutes later, a spread of pancakes, eggs, bacon, sausage, country ham, French toast, hash browns, an assortment of fruit, and her mother's signature breakfast casserole filled the table. Just as everyone made their way to the dining room to sit down, Alyssa walked in. She spoke to and hugged their parents, then her sisters and nephew. Everyone sat down after a few minutes and Abraham said grace.

"What a pleasant surprise. All of our girls and nephew under one roof. All we missing is more babies and husbands. Speaking of husbands, where's Richard?" Abraham sat at the head of the table and spoke as everyone began eating.

"He had a business meeting, he'll be back later," Anastasia said while the other sisters silently grumbled at the husband comment.

Andrea looked up just in time to notice Alyssa and Anastasia share a look that said something more was going on than what Anastasia shared with the family. She also noticed how Alyssa kept checking her phone and sending texts, which confirmed that she had just flat out ignored her earlier. Andrea reached for her mom's casserole that she loved so much and scooped some onto her plate. As soon as she lifted the fork to her mouth to take a bite, she felt queasy again. She rushed to the bathroom and barely made it once again, and emptied what felt like her entire stomach.

"What the fuck is wrong wit me?" she mumbled to herself.

"You alright, sweetheart?" Mr. Holiday asked from the other side of the door because she had closed it as soon as he made it, not wanting to be bothered.

"I'm fine dad. I think it was something I ate yesterday that didn't agree with me," Drea told him.

"Okay… just checking on you," he replied and she heard his footsteps as he walked away.

Once again, Andrea washed her face and brushed her teeth. The feeling of annoyance was slowly taking over her because she wasn't one to get sick often. Andrea hadn't been to the doctor for any type of sickness in at least five or six years and that was for food poisoning. She was beginning to feel like she had been food poisoned again.

"Get it together, Drea," she said to herself in the mirror, then made her way back to the dining room.

All eyes were on Andrea as she walked back in. She already knew that she was about to hear some comments, so she braced herself.

"Drea, that's the second time this morning… no more drinks for you," Lexi blurted out.

"Second time? I would say she was pregnant, but we all know she ain't getting none," Anastasia mumbled, but Drea heard her loud and clear.

"Drinks? None of y'all need to be drinking," Mr. Holiday chimed in.

"Here it goes, like we all babies," Alyssa mumbled.

"We ain't been together a good hour and y'all already at each other's throats. Stop it," Mrs. Holiday demanded.

"Whelp, it was fun while it lasted. Lexi and Stasia y'all can do the dishes," Drea pointed out.

"Why you can't do em?" Stasia challenged.

"Girl, come do these dishes. She cooked," Lexi said and winked at Andrea.

Mrs. Holiday got up and made her way to the kitchen while singing *We've Come This Far By Faith* while Mr. Holiday headed to his study. Nothing in the Holiday home had changed amongst the parents, it was the children who switched up and decided not to visit home as promised. At times, Andrea wanted to move away, but who would be around to check on their aging parents if she left? That was the question that always popped into her head and made her quickly dismiss the thought. Andrea went into the kitchen and grabbed a ginger ale out of the fridge and took about three swallows. She said a silent prayer that the queasiness would not return because she didn't have time for it.

Alexis and Anastasia were in the kitchen doing the dishes, fussing as usual, and Andrea chuckled as she walked out. She walked to Alyssa'a old room and found her on the phone again.

"Your fiancé dumped you and won't answer? You been in that phone ever since you made it," Andrea startled Alyssa and said.

"Huh… what?" Alyssa stuttered.

"If you can huh you can hear? You thought that ring was gonna go unnoticed? What's going on wit you?" Drea fired question after question at Alyssa.

"Drea, you're so fuckin nosey and never give anybody time to tell you anything. I guess the lawyer in you just gotta investigate and point out shit," Alyssa rolled her eyes.

"Well damn… all I asked was about your ring and how you showed up not paying attention to shit, but your phone. Rude ass," Drea fired back, then turned to leave.

"Wait Drea… my bad. I ain't tryna fuss wit you this weekend. I got some news Ima share with the whole family later, okay," Alyssa reasoned with her.

"Okay Lyssa… cool, but I'm sure Stasia knows," Drea said and shook her head.

She heard Alyssa saying that she was sure Lexi knew all of her secrets, too, but she ignored her and kept going. It was about to be time to start preparing dinner for the next day, so Drea decided to go and talk to her dad until her other sisters finished cleaning up. She had a few things that that she needed to get off her chest and there was no better time than the present.

Chapter 23

After a four-hour flight, the Uber pulled up to The Holiday residence and Alyssa saw that the front door was open. The driver popped the trunk and got out and grabbed her bags. Alyssa retrieved them and headed towards the house. Walking up the porch steps, the smell of bacon hit her nose causing her stomach to growl. Alyssa opened the screen door and entered the house. She sat her suitcases by the door as she listened to the chatter that was coming from the dining room. She hung her jacket up on the coat rack before she made her way to her family and made it just in time for breakfast. Alyssa tried not to seem too distant at the table, but she couldn't stay off her phone. She locked eyes with Andrea for a brief moment and the look she gave her told her to put her phone away and she complied.

Andrea got a little sick during breakfast, but Alyssa almost missed it because she was too preoccupied with her phone. Her big sister quickly got herself together and told Alexis and Anastasia to wash the breakfast dishes. Anastasia fussed a little, but eventually gave in. Once they were done, the women began preparing the food for Thanksgiving dinner. Victoria assigned all the sisters a dish to prepare. Victoria monitored the girls for a few minutes before she left out leaving Andrea in charge like always. As soon as she was gone, the girls didn't hesitate to start clowning each other.

"I hope y'all heffas remember how to cook. I don't want to have to go behind y'all and make everything all over again," Andrea stated from the counter.

"Hmmm. That statement must have been for Lexi because she's struggling with them greens," Anastasia chuckled.

"Did you wash those off first?" Stasia quizzed.

"You have to wash them off?" Lexi asked.

They all burst into laughter.

"Fuck y'all hoes," Alexis pouted as she made her way over to the sink with the greens.

"Leave her alone, y'all. Y'all act like y'all always knew how to cook. How many times have you fucked up the food, Lyssa?" Andrea looked and smirked.

"Why you bringing up old shit, Drea? Alyssa rolled her eyes.

"Don't trip, Lyssa. Miss perfect ain't always know how to cook either. Besides, you should've known she wasn't going to let us get away with making fun of baby sis," Anastasia chimed in.

"Don't start with the bullshit," Andrea said with a stern tone.

"Bitch, you ain't scaring nobody." Alyssa dismissed her.

"Aight, girls. Behave yourselves," Mr. Holiday scolded as he entered the kitchen. "I'm glad y'all are here, but I want y'all to keep the bickering to a minimum. Do y'all hear me?"

They murmured in agreement.

"Good. I'm about to go. I have a counseling session over at the church. Can I expect to see y'all at bible study tonight? It starts at seven," he glanced around the kitchen at the girls.

They all looked at each other before their eyes landed on Andrea to answer their fathers' question.

"Daddy, we can't make bible study tonight, but we'll be at church on Sunday. We wanna spend some alone time catching up," Andrea smiled.

"I guess I'll let y'all slide," he smiled. "Remember what I told y'all and keep an eye on Alyssa and make sure she doesn't mess up that macaroni and cheese," he teased.

Everyone laughed except Alyssa.

"That's not funny, Dad."

"You know I'm just messing with you, sweetie." He kissed her cheek. "I'll see y'all later."

"Bye, Dad," they said in unison.

After their dad left, the girls discussed what they were going to do after they finished preparing the food and Andrea suggested that they go to a place called Last Call and they all agreed. Alyssa wasn't really in the mood to party, but she figured that she could turn up with her sisters in hopes that it would take her mind off Corey.

They spent hours joking each other and cooking. When they were finished with the dinner and desserts, Alyssa grabbed her luggage and carried them up to her old room. She unpacked her suitcase and decided on an outfit to wear for the night before she hopped into the shower. She washed her body a few times before washing her face and brushing her teeth. When she was finished in the bathroom, she laid down for a little while. She texted and called Corey again, all to no avail, then she scrolled through Facebook, Snap Chat, and Instagram for a little while. When Alyssa got bored, she noticed that it was almost eight o'clock, so she went ahead and got dressed. Once she was dressed, she put on her Jimmy Choo heels and rose gold accessories. Alyssa checked herself out in the mirror, took a few photos and sent them to Corey. She didn't expect him to respond, but she figured it wouldn't hurt to remind him what he was missing out on.

Alyssa removed her ID and credit card from her wallet and slid them in her cell phone case which was also a wallet. She put her jacket on before she went downstairs, so her mother wouldn't see her outfit. Alyssa was rocking a black one-piece pantsuit that exposed her stomach and back and even though she was grown, she knew her mother was going to give her an earful about her outfit. Her sisters were in the kitchen with their jackets on as well as they made small talk with their mother. When they saw Alyssa, they quickly kissed their mother good-bye and rushed out the door.

They all piled into Andreas' car and instantly took off their jackets. Andrea crunk up, and Lexi turned the volume up on the radio as Drea pulled off. They nodded their heads to *Slippery* by Gucci Mane featuring Migos as they made their way to the club. Alyssa pulled out her phone and posted their turn up on Snapchat. Minutes later, they were pulling into the parking lot and Andrea parked in the first spot she saw. They hopped out the car and strutted towards the entrance of the club like they owned the place. A couple of men that were standing in the front of the line pulled Alexis by the hand and allowed her to get in front of them. Her sisters followed suit and seconds later, they were inside. They made their way through the party goers on the dance floor over to the bar. For it to be early, there were quite a few people out already. Alyssa assumed because it was the holiday weekend.

"Aight y'all. What we drinking?" Alexis asked as she sat down.

"Let's do some shots," Anastasia answered.

"Are you sure you need to drink again?" Lexi quizzed.

"I'm good. First round on Alyssa," Andrea added.

"That's cool with me," she pulled out her credit card.

Andrea ordered four double shots of peach Ciroc and waited a few seconds for the bartender to hand her their drinks. After paying for the drinks, the girls took a glass, counted to three and tossed the drinks back. They ordered another round of shots and tossed those back before they made their way to the dance floor. *No Limit* by G-Easy featuring Cardi B came through the speakers of the club and the girls found a nigga to grind on. As they twerked to the music, Alyssa couldn't help but notice how Alexis was dancing. She was bouncing and popping her ass like she was performing for a rap video. Alyssa locked eyes with her sisters and they were just as shocked as she was.

Alyssa danced for a few songs before she made her way to the bathroom. There was a short line, but that didn't bother her. A few minutes later, she handled her business and used her foot to flush the toilet. She washed her hands, grabbed a paper towel and tossed it in the trash. When she was leaving out, someone was coming in and almost hit her with the door. Alyssa jumped back and fixed her lips to cuss the bitch out, but when she realized that it was Alexis's best friend, Bre, she eased up.

"Hey Bre. Long time no see, girl."

"Hey Lyssa," she hugged her.

"What you doing back in Mississippi?" Bre asked.

"I came home to spend time with the family for the holidays. All of my sisters are here," Alyssa replied.

"Really? Even Lexi?" Bre quizzed with a face of confusion.

"Yup. You should come to our house tomorrow for dinner," Alyssa offered.

"I'd love to have dinner with y'all. What time should I be there?" Bre beamed.

"Around three," Alyssa confirmed.

"Cool. See you tomorrow," Alyssa said and walked off.

Alyssa heard Bre mumble something under her breath before she walked out of the bathroom, but decided to ignore it. She found her sisters sitting at a table and Alyssa was happy that there was food on the table. She noticed that Lexi wasn't at the table and asked her sisters where she was because she was about to tell her that she had just saw her best friend. Anastasia told her that Lexi left. Alyssa wondered where the hell her baby sister was going, but decided to leave it alone. They had buffalo wings, which was her favorite, waiting for her. They made small talk while they ate and had a few more drinks.

The remaining sisters left the club around one o'clock. Alyssa asked Andrea if she was cool to drive and she confirmed with a head nod. She could tell the wheels were turning in Andrea's head, but she decided not to speak on it. As they drove home in silence, Alyssa checked her phone to see if Corey had texted her and he had. She read his message and smile. Her man would be there in the morning to spend Thanksgiving with her and her family.

Chapter 24

Surprisingly, the first two days back at home actually went by smoothly. Lexi stayed with Drea the very first day and the next day she spent time with her parents and other sisters, which was shockingly fun. Lexi knew not to get ahead of herself because although things was starting off good, she knew how her sisters got down and that shit could go from 0 to 100 real quick.

"You been smiling and texting all damn day. How do you expect to enjoy yourself with that phone in your hand?" Drea scolded loudly over the music playing at Last Call.

"I'm texting J.R. Remember I told you that he was going out of town to Louisiana? Well turns out that him and his people staying at a hotel about one hour away from here and he want to see me." Lexi beamed.

"Girl no.... HELL NO! We having sister time. You might as well call him and tell him you not coming." Andrea order. Lexi looked at her sister and screwed up her face before grabbing her phone to read the message that just came in from J.R.

"Welp! Too late, he outside. I gotta go. Peacccceeee out!" she yelled, grabbing her Chanel clutch off the seat next to her and standing to her feet. "Tell them other hoes, I'm gone." Lexi continued, as she pulled down the tight black body-con dress she was wearing, before exiting their section and leaving the lounge.

When she made it outside, the crisp Mississippi wind crept up her dress, causing goosebumps to form all over her skin. Her eyes searched the street until they landed on J.R.'s all-white Mercedes G Wagon. Once he noticed her, the doors opened up and he stepped out wearing a pair of Balmain jeans, a cream Moncler coat and some Navy blue and white Mikes. A huge smile invaded her face before she took off in his directions, damn near running. He watched her as she crossed the street dodging between cars just to get to him.

"What's up, baby?" he said, greeting her first. Lexi ran right into his arms while he picked her up slightly off the ground, hugging her tight. "You act like you miss daddy," he boasted before letting her go. Lexi didn't respond, she walked around to the passenger side of the car and got in.

"You know I miss you, but it's obvious you miss me, too," she cooed.

"I don't know about all that, shorty," he replied, laughing before peeling off from the curb.

"You can stunt all you want, but I know you do. How's business been going?" she asked, adjusting her ass in the heated seats.

"Aw business went well. How's the family shit going?" He looked over briefly at Lexi and asked before looking back at the road.

Lexi took a deep breath before replying, "So far, so good. I haven't told you, but I only get along with one of my sisters and that's the oldest, Drea. My other two sisters, Stasia and Lyssa, I love them to death, but those hoes get on my nerves. It's always been a tag-team thing ever since we was little, but it's cool."

"What about your parents, they straight?"

"They just happy that we all under the same roof. I'm trying my best to keep the peace, just for them," Lexi explained.

"Yeah, I get that. How they feel about your career choice?" J.R. asked followed a light chuckle.

Lexi wasn't sure if he was throwing shade or truly wanted to know. "Nobody knows; my father is a pastor."

"A PASTOR? GET THE FUCK OUTTA HERE!" he hollered. "Aw wait, you dead ass huh?" he continued, noticing that nothing about Lexi's tone hinted that she was joking.

"Yeah, I know; it's crazy, right?" she finally said, looking out the window.

"I swear, baby. I only be hearing about shit like this in those movies where buddy ass be wearing the dresses acting like an old woman."

"You mean, Madea?" Lexi asked.

"Yeah. Yeah. Yeah. That nigga movies. I ain't never met a motherfucker in real life who truly going through that shit," he stated.

"It's more to it than you know, but enough about my dysfunctional life. Where you taking me? Where we going?" she asked.

"I'm kidnapping you tonight. We booked some rooms at this hotel up the road. You spending the night with me," he confirmed.

"Awwww… so you asking me or telling me?" she quizzed.

"I'm telling you. We finna go to the room and I'm finna fuck the shit out of the Pastor's daughter and we gon chill.," J.R. said, causing both him and Lexi to laugh.

After driving for about another thirty minutes, they pulled into the parking lot of The Residence Inn by Marriot. J.R. lucked up on a park right in front. He pulled into the spot, killed the engine, and got out. Lexi followed his lead and did the same, walking towards the double glass doors.

"What you got on this lil shit for?" J.R. asked, smacking Lexi on the ass, causing it to jiggle.

She turned around and blew him an air kiss before heading to the front desk of the hotel. J.R. checked them in while Lexi stood off to the side on her phone. She texted Drea, letting her know that she made it to her destination safely and not to wait up for her. Lexi locked her phone and attempted to put it back in her clutch when it fell and hit the floor.

"Dear father God, please don't let my screen be cracked when I turn it over. In Jesus name, Amen!" Lexi's prayers were answered when she bent down to retrieve her phone. "Look at God," she said to herself before securing her phone safely this time.

"Here bae, gone upstairs, I gotta get my charger out the car," J.R. said, handing Lexi the key card to the room. She took the card and headed towards the elevator when she felt her phone vibrating in her bag. She knew that it was Drea texting her back, but when she grabbed it, she had a text from Bre.

Bestfriend Bre: I hope you having a good time in New York. I miss you, can't wait til you get back home. I love u ☺

Lexi rolled her eyes before tossing her phone back in her bag. Although her read receipts were on, she didn't give a fuck about Bre's crazy ass. Lexi had every intention of moving when she got back to Atlanta. She knew that dealing with Bre was toxic and she needed to be as far away from her as possible.

Lexi pressed the up arrow on the elevator and waited for it to reach her level.

"Ooohh girl, your shoes are so cute," a lady said, walking up to Lexi, waiting on the elevator as well.

"Thank you!" Lexi replied with a warm smile.

Seconds later, the elevator arrived and both women stepped on. Lexi pressed the number five button, requesting that floor. As soon as the doors began to close, a male voice called out for them to hold the elevator.

"My slow ass man, I'm sorry girl," The lady apologized as she stopped the doors from closing with her arms.

Lexi didn't say anything, instead she acknowledged what she said with a smile; however, her smile quickly faded when the woman's man joined them on the elevator. Lexi and Richard locked eyes and at that moment, Lexi could literally see the life exiting his body.

"Hey brother!" Lexi cheerfully said, staring at Richard up and down.

"Baby, you know her?" the unknown woman asked.

"Of course, he knows me; ain't that right, BROTHER?" Lexi replied.

"Ummm... ye...yeah I – I- I know her. She's my sister," Richard stuttered.

"Really? I didn't know you had a sister. What a small world," the dense blonde bitch replied.

"Tell me about it. Well ya'll enjoy ya'll night," Lexi stated once the elevator stopped on her floor.

"We on this floor, too. Oh my God, this night is getting freakier by the second," Richard's chick stated.

"This night ain't shit; watch how things turn up tomorrow. Ain't that right, BROTHER?" Lexi yelled one last time before she went left, while Richard and lil mama went right.

Lexi pulled out her phone to text Drea to let her know how Anastasia's husband was just caught red handed, but decided that she rather see her facial expression when she got served this tea. Their parents bragged about Stasia being the only one married and boasted on how happy they were, although everybody else knew that it was fraudulent as fuck. Lexi was just happy that she had the proof and she couldn't wait to throw the shit in that bougie bitch's face.

Chapter 25

Anastasia woke up the next morning thankful that she didn't have a hangover. She glanced over at a still sleeping Kyler and eased out the bed, grabbing her phone from the nightstand at the same time. She'd been calling and messaging Richard all night to find out what time he would be arriving to her parent's house, but his ass hadn't responded at all. Of course, she really wasn't too worried because his sleeping schedule was just as boring as his clothes. On any given day, he was in bed by at least 9, so it wasn't too unusual that he hadn't answered. It was going on 8 o'clock and even though she knew that he was up, he still hadn't acknowledged her messages. Grumbling under her breath, she shuffled into the bathroom and handled her hygiene noting that no one appeared to be up yet. She figured that since she was the first one woke, she would get breakfast started for everyone.

Once she was done in the bathroom, she headed downstairs and into the kitchen with her head still down into her phone.

"Shit!"

She looked up to see Alexis who'd been trying to creep into the back door with an annoyed look on her face. Anastasia instantly felt a smile spread across her lips. Guess little miss Alexis wasn't so perfect after all.

"You know the only thing open this time of morning is 7/11 and legs?" she teased and Alexis's face balled up into an even deeper frown.

"I wonder which one is the reason you're creepin in here," Anastasia taunted.

"Bitch, you should be askin your husband the same thing," she replied smartly, making sure to bump her sister's shoulder as she walked past.

Anastasia's smile dropped, but before she could say anything Lexi was already gone. She knew that Richard staying at the hotel was going to be a mistake. Her sisters didn't miss shit, but Lexi's assumption was all wrong. Anastasia would admit that Richard was an asshole, but he wouldn't cheat. Would he?

Shaking her head, Anastasia proceeded to the refrigerator to pull out the necessary items for breakfast. Her sister was just trying to get in her head because of some old hating shit and they didn't get along. It had always been that way. Lexi and Drea cliqued up against Lyssa and herself. Regardless of the charade they were all putting up for the holidays, it would probably always be that way, so she shrugged her shoulders and let the comment go.

Not wanting to get too extra with breakfast, she only pulled out eggs, bacon, and some biscuits. Once she set everything on the table, she checked her phone once again relieved to see that Richard had sent a text saying he'd be on his way shortly. She couldn't help but let out a sigh of relief that he would be there soon and stop any questions on his whereabouts. Sitting the phone back down, she smiled as Lyssa walked into the kitchen already dressed.

"Morning sis. What made you start breakfast today?" she asked, heading to the refrigerator and pulling out a banana and some yogurt.

"Good morning and shit, I figured I might as well since Andrea did yesterday," she shrugged, noticing the food in her sister's hand.

"You goin' somewhere?" she queried.

"Yeah girl," she sighed with a dreamy smile.

"Corey is on the way and I have to pick him up from the airport."

Anastasia was glad that she seemed more excited about being married to Corey. The last thing she wanted was for her to feel trapped in a marriage like she was. Corey being successful and the two actually wanting to be together was a major plus for her. It was obvious that being with him gave her a glow and she could only pray that they continued on the path that they were on.

"I'm glad he's comin' girl, that way daddy will stay off your back," Anastasia rolled her eyes dramatically.

"I know, right? Girl, the last thing I need is him bothering me about anything. At least with Corey here, daddy will only talk shit to them other bitches," they both laughed and shared a high-five.

"I swear he need to fuck with them a lil bit more hell! I just caught Lexi lil thot ass sneakin in here," Anastasia said, causing Lyssa's eyes to buck, but before she could say anything the doorbell rang. The sisters shared a look, both wondering who would be there so early when their mom's sister, Aunt Shirley's voice filled the house.

"Where the hell all ya'll at?" she hollered just before entering the kitchen.

Anastasia held in her laugh as she took in the sight before her. Aunt Shirley stood swaying in the doorway wearing a long red moo moo looking dress with flowers all over it. One of the off-white knee highs she wore was all the way up, while the other was rolled down to her ankles and the black geriatric shoes looked run over. It was obvious she had already been drinking by the way her wig sat on her head; if the flask she was clutching wasn't a dead giveaway.

"And that's my cue," Alyssa muttered, taking her food and heading out of the kitchen. Anastasia grumbled under her breath, but she would curse her ass out later.

"Uh, I know you gone speak to yo favorite Aunty before you walk out of here!" Aunt Shirley slurred, placing her free hand on her wide hips.

"Of course, not Aunt Shirley," she said through her teeth with a fake smile, and threw her arms around Aunt's shoulders while making a face at Anastasia.

When the embrace ended, Alyssa mouthed good luck once Aunt Shirley turned back to Anastasia with a frown. She didn't speak, she only stared her down while she scrambled the eggs in a bowl.

"Yes, Aunt Shirley?" she asked without lifting her head.

"You gone give me some love, too or you gone just continue to pretend I ain't standin' here?"

With a deep sigh, Anastasia sat the fork she was using down and made her way over to hug her, even though the last thing she wanted to do was be in breathing room of her.

"Sorry Aunty."

As soon as she was close enough, Anastasia held her breath against the strong stench of vodka that was emanating from her dear Aunt. She quickly released herself from the hold she had on her and went back over to the food she was preparing before her Aunt came in.

"Where everybody else at and why the hell you down here cookin' breakfast? Ain't Thanksgiving tomorrow? Ya'll should be getting the food ready for tomorrow's dinner, not makin this shit!" she complained with a frown.

Anastasia looked up at her in irritation and tried to force down the insult that was threatening to spill out. It was a wonder she could even understand what she'd said between the slur and that country ass accent. It was Thanksgiving Day and her drunk ass aunt was standing there saying it was the next day.

"Everybody is still upstairs sleep and daddy bout to run to the church in a minute Aunt Shirley, and I'm cooking breakfast because that's what normal people eat in the morning. And we're actually eating Thanksgiving dinner TODAY at three," she said sweetly, then added under her breath. "Old vodka drinking ass can't keep up with the days."

"Humph! Well, me and ya mama didn't cook breakfast on Thanksgiving Day when we was younger."

"It's been a long ass time since you been young," Anastasia grumbled, turning her back and putting the eggs in the pan to fry. Before they could bubble, she hurried to put the pan of butter in the oven to melt, so that she could cook the bacon.

"I heard that!"

"I didn't even say anything, Aunt Shirley," she lied, quickly glancing back to take in the sight of her auntie. She took a sip of her flask before flopping down into one of the chairs at the table and setting a hard stare on Anastasia.

"Girl, you as bad at lyin' as you is in that fraud ass marriage!" she laughed loudly. "Where Richard's ass at anyway, Anastasia?"

Anastasia's shoulders stiffened at the comment and she turned around to give her a piece of her mind when her mama entered the kitchen saving her.

"Shirley!" she shrieked, happiness was evident in her voice at the sight of her sister.

Anastasia watched as her Aunt stumbled to her feet, so that they could hug and wondered if her mama was gonna say something about her reeking of alcohol.

"Sista, you know I was comin to see my family; especially, these lovely girls," Aunty Shirley gushed like she hadn't been just sitting there insulting her.

With an eye roll, Anastasia turned back to the stove and finished the eggs, placing them into a bowl and sitting them on the table. They continued to make small talk for another minute before her mother finally turned her attention to Anastasia.

"Baby, thank you for making breakfast." She gave her a kiss on the cheek as she stood at the counter preparing the biscuits for the oven.

"It's no problem, mama. I was already up," Anastasia explained, putting one of her arms around her mother's waist and laying her head on her shoulder.

"Well, I appreciate it," she lamented.

"Will Richard be joining us this morning?" She wanted to know and her Aunt burst into laughter behind them, causing them both to turn around.

"Oh, my bad. I thought that was in my head," she lied and took another drink. Anastasia rolled her eyes and went back to the task at hand, while her mother looked on at her Aunt in disapproval.

"Shirley, I thought you were slowin' down on the liquor; you shouldn't even be drinking this early," she scolded. "You know Abraham is not gone want you drinkin in here."

"First of all, I'm the big sister and our mama is dead and second of all, Fuck Abraham!" she snapped, taking another sip. "He the one that gotta live by the word. Jesus know my heart! And he know that I'ma need this to get through the holidays."

Anastasia choked on spit trying to hold in her laughter as her mother gasped in shock. Even though her Aunt was a pain in the ass at times, she damn sure was gonna make it easier being there during the holidays. They continued to go back and forth as Anastasia swapped out the bacon in the oven for the biscuits. Of course, her mother won the argument and her Aunt Shirley put her drink away, but she was sure that she'd finished it all by that time.

She knew once her father and sisters came down, it would be even more arguing and insults, but Anastasia was there for it; especially, if it took the heat off her and Richard's situation. At least their dad would be gone shortly. Aunt Shirley continued to sit and talk mess while Anastasia and her mom set the table.

"I hope the whole time I'm here you don't want me puttin on airs for yo husband and shit," she huffed and smacked her lips.

"Shirley, I'm not bout to play with you. You don't need to put on airs for nobody! We all know you're a damn drunk, but WE, me and Abraham, would appreciate it if you would be sober for one day," Mama said, reading Aunt Shirley for filth. Unable to argue after that, she elected to just be quiet as Anastasia fixed her plate. "Now, eat this food so you can sober up a lil before everybody comes down here," Mama said sternly, sitting the plate in front of her and walking away. Lexi came down right after that in some pajamas like her ass had just woke up and Anastasia rolled her eyes.

"Good morning everybody," she cheesed, giving Anastasia, a look daring her to say something.

Anastasia smirked in her direction, even though she had no intentions on telling in the first place. Satisfied that she wouldn't have to start no shit, Alexis kissed both her aunt and mother before taking a seat at the table.

"Hey, Lexi chile! I heard you been hittin' them books hard baby; good for you," Aunt Shirley complimented with a smile.

"Aww yeah, Aunty. You know how I does it," Lexi gushed as their mama sat a plate in front of her.

"Mmm hmmm… Now, if you hit the books as hard as you do the club, then you should be valedictorian," she said and took a bite of her eggs causing Lexi to choke on the orange juice she was drinking.

"Shirley, leave her alone! You can't stop being messy for five damn seconds!" Aunt Shirley waved her off and continued to eat like she hadn't said anything wrong.

"I'm gonna go get Kyler, ma. Do you mind calling Drea over?" Anastasia asked over her shoulder as she headed out of the kitchen. She took the stairs two at a time and found him still asleep. Giving him a gentle shake, he woke right up with a smile.

"Good morning, baby."

"Good morning, ma." He sat up in bed and rubbed his eyes sleepily.

"Come on, let's wash your face and brush your teeth so that you can eat."

With ease, he got out of bed and grabbed his toothbrush out of his bag. Anastasia handed him one of the towels from the linen closet and watched as he went into the bathroom to handle his hygiene while she called his father.

"I'm coming, Ana," he answered and he already sounded irritated. She sucked her teeth at his tone, but decided not to comment on it.

"Good morning to you, too, Richard," she said sarcastically. "I was actually only calling to ask if you were going to make it for breakfast."

"I'll be there in the next ten minutes I'm already turning the corner."

"Well, alright, I'll see you then," she replied, but realized that he had already hung up.

Anastasia pulled the phone from her ear and frowned at it. Richard had really gotten beside himself with the disrespect. She would have preferred to put him in his place at home, but if he kept this shit up, she was going to go off on his ass. Sighing, she helped Kyler finish up in the bathroom before they both went down to breakfast.

When she made it back into the kitchen, she was pleased to see Richard at the table and she was even more pleased to see that her Aunt Shirley was getting in his ass about his absence. He looked up as she entered, hoping that she would help him, but she ignored his ass and went to make Kyler a plate.

"Don't look at Anastasia, she can't help you," Aunty Shirley tisked until she noticed Kyler beside her.

"Oh, hey baby, I'm aunt Shirley! I heard so much about you! Come give yo aunty a hug sugar!" she gushed like she wasn't coming for his father just a second before.

Everybody greeted him with hugs and kisses and Richard let out a sigh of relief that her focus was off of him. Anastasia was still a little irritated by him, but that didn't stop her from giving him a kiss on the cheek and murmuring good morning. He smiled just like he was supposed to and gave her a kiss back before greeting their son.

"Hey big man," he reached out to Kyler and rubbed the top of his head as he took a seat on one side of him while Anastasia sat down on the other.

"Hey dad," was his dry response.

Anastasia noticed the looks everyone shared making note of how their son had greeted him and instantly went into damage control mode.

"He's not really a morning person," she excused him.

Her mom and Aunt Shirley both nodded their understanding while Lexi rolled her eyes with a grunt. It figured that she would be the one who wouldn't just accept what she said.

"Lexi, you look pretty well rested considering how you just got in not too long ago." she said putting her on the spot. Everyone's eyes went to Lexi as she gulped down the forkful of eggs she'd just eaten.

"Alexis Holiday! What were you doing out all night?" their mother asked.

"Probably at one of them clubs! I know I sholl be tryna get in them after hours spots," Aunt Shirley added her two cents and Anastasia rolled her eyes.

"Actually mom," Lexi dragged, shooting daggers at Anastasia.

"I slept next door with Drea. Maybe Stasia should concern herself with her husband's whereabouts and stay out my business," Anastasia looked over at Richard with her brows knitted.

That was the second time that Alexis had made mention of him like he was doing things he wasn't supposed to. She noted the look he gave Lexi before glancing at her with a shrug.

"Oh ok, well that's fine then. Anastasia, please stop trying to dry snitch," their mother scolded lightly.

"Where is Andrea anyway?" Mrs. Holiday asked.

"She's still sleeping mom, I don't think she's feeling good," Lexi said, finally getting back to her food.

"And Lyssa?"

"Oh, she went to pick up Corey from the airport," Anastasia piped up, finally taking her eyes off of Richard.

"Well, your father will be pleased to see him here once he returns from the church. At least we know two of you are settling down."

"More like just settling," Lexi grumbled and Anastasia threw her a look, but didn't say anything. She'd already wiggled her way out of the shade Anastasia had thrown; she didn't want to spend the morning taking shots.

They all finished breakfast without any more insults, surprisingly, and after they finished, Stasia and Lexi washed the dishes. Their mama and Aunt didn't take any time taking things out to begin prepping dinner while they cleaned and Richard went to help Kyler get dressed. Anastasia said a silent prayer as her and Lexi washed the dishes in silence, that the remainder of the trip would not be full of drama.

Chapter 26

Lexi knew when she heard Auntie Shirley's voice, shit was finna be cracking. Shirley was her favorite auntie and everybody swore on their life that that was how Lexi was going to act once she got her age. Aunt Shirley didn't have a filter and neither did Lexi, which was probably why when everybody else was busy being offended by the things she said, Lexi dusted that shit off and went about her business.

"How was the breakfast, baby?" Mrs. Holiday asked her youngest child.

"Who made it?" Lexi questioned, while looking around at everybody in the kitchen.

"I did… why?" Stasia replied, rolling her neck.

"Well, in that case, the eggs were burnt, the bacon wasn't done, and the biscuits was dry," Lexi laughed before going to the sink, tossing her plate in. Anastasia smacked her lips and rolled her eyes while their mother giggled.

"The princess of shade has arisen," Auntie Shirley stated before sneaking a sip from her flask while Mrs. Holiday head was turned.

"Play nice, Alexis! I need you to run to the store to get some cranberry sauce and a case of water, but first help your sister with the dishes." Mrs. Holiday ordered.

Lexi helped out with the dishes, when she was done, she stopped next door to Drea's house to make sure that she covered for her if anyone asked where she was last night. After speaking briefly with her, Lexi made her first stop at Walmart. To her surprise, the store was packed. For some silly reason, she had this idea that everyone was done shopping at that point and was at home cooking, but she thought wrong. Not wanting to be in the store long and being bothered with all the people, Lexi headed straight to the back to the grocery section and grabbed three jars of cranberry sauce and a 24 pack of Aquafina water.

"Let me help you with that, Baby Holiday." She heard a voice say from behind her. Lexi lifted the water before turning around, greeting the person who called her by a name she hated so much.

"Oh my God! Hey Zyree," Lexi smiled, speaking to an old friend. It had been a few years since she last seen him. Zyree was Anastasia's first love before she got wrapped all up into Richard's trifling ass. He was a good man, but their parents hated him, so of course, things didn't work out in his favor.

"How have you been? Little Lexi is all grown up now," he replied.

"I've been good. I live in Atlanta now," she said, handing him the case of water he reached for as the both of them headed to the register.

"Oh word? You here for the holidays, huh?" he asked.

"Yup and so is my sister, wink wink," Lexi replied, winking her right eye noticeably at Zyree. He laughed as he sat the case of water, along with his items on the belt, sending them in the direction of the cashier.

"Man, I haven't seen Stasia's fine ass in years. Last time I heard, she was married."

"Married…. Married…. Married…. Who cares? What I do think is, you should stop by today and visit,"

Lexi beamed at the idea of Zyree showing up at dinner while Richard was there.

A part of Lexi was starting to feel bad. She should have told Stasia the moment she saw her husband last night, but all the sneak dissing and shade being thrown made her reconsider. She felt that if she invited Zyree, then Richard would see that Stasia had other options. That was Lexi's way of making things better.

"I can't! I gotta make a move later on tonight, but thanks for the invite and tell everyone, especially Stasia, that I said hey." Zyree said, flashing that million-dollar smile.

"Aight! Well at least shoot her a text or something, here's her number," Lexi replied, while she grabbed her phone, pulling up Stasia's contact info and reading it off to Zyree.

He put the number in his phone before promising to call and leaving the store. Lexi grabbed her things and walked behind him, heading to Drea's car. Once she threw the things inside, she then pulled her phone back out, sending a text to her homie, Cam, letting him know she was five minutes away. Lexi pulled up to Cam's house and luckily for her, he was already out front. She put the car in park, never turning off the engine before blowing the horn two times. Cam bent down to make sure it was her in the car before making his way towards her.

"Sexy Lexi, what's up beautiful?" he said, smiling from the driver's side window.

"What up?" she replied dryly, before digging in her purse pulling out $40.00 in cash.

"You got my shit?" she asked, handing him the money, then quickly snatching it back.

"You know I do. This shit here fye, too." Cam confirmed, handing Lexi a zip lock bag with some kush inside.

"It better be or Imma kick yo fat ass, Cam," she said jokingly, securing the weed in her purse.

"Ohhhh baby, don't play me like that," he oozed, staring at her breast.

"Thanks Cam. Bye Cam," Lexi responded, putting her car in drive and pulling off before he could say anything else.

Lexi made a quick stop at the gas station, grabbing a few packs of white peach swishers and heading back towards the house. She pulled in front instead of in Drea's driveway and killed the engine before heading inside. Lexi grabbed the bag and case of water and brought them along with her. When she walked in, her mother and aunt was still at the table preparing things for dinner.

"It took you long enough," Aunt Shirley said, cutting her eyes at Lexi.

"I had to make an additional stop, I mean if that's ok with you," Lexi snapped.

"Oooohhhh girrrrrrllll… Yo mouth gon get yo ass beat," Aunt Shirley snapped back.

"First of all, stop cursing in my house and stop threatening my child," Mrs. Holiday said before walking over to the stove placing the pies inside.

"Meet me outside," Lexi whispered to her aunt before heading out the door. Lexi went back outside and sat in Drea's car. Moments later, her Aunt Shirley was opening up the door and joining her.

"I ever tell you that you my favorite?" Aunt Shirley said, getting comfortable in the leather seats.

"Yea, you only tell me that when you smoking up my weed," Lexi replied, breaking down the blunt.

"Nah, this just how we bond. You see I can't bond with your other sisters. Them heffas too damn bougie for me, but you, you remind me of myself when I was growing up," she rambled on.

Lexi rolled her eyes and continued to prepare for the smoke session that her and Aunt Shirley was about to have. The only reason she included her was so she can keep her mouth shut. Ever since Lexi started sneaking and smoking, Aunt Shirley seemed to be the only person who noticed when she was high.

"So, how's school going?" she asked, taking her first pull from the blunt.

"It's going good. This my last year, so I'm happy about that," she replied, smiling from the thought of graduation as well at the fact that J.R. sent her a text.

"You are coming back home, right?" she quizzed.

"Nah, most likely not……. Auntie hand me my purse from by your feet," Lexi requested.

"Girrrlll this nice. What kind of purse is this?"

"It's a Birkin bag," Lexi replied.

"Girl where the fuck are you getting money from to afford things like this. Now, I know it cost a lot because I hear all them rappers talking about it," Her auntie stated.

"I paid for it."

"How? What you robbing banks?" Shirley asked in a serious tone.

"Nah lady," Lexi said, waving her off.

"Well, you doing something. I don't know why you and your sisters so secretive. I keep telling ya'll that what's done in the dark will eventually come to the light, but ya'll keep thinking that I'm an old fool if ya want to," she preached.

Lexi didn't bother to reply. Instead, she finished up the blunt with her aunt and listened to her ramble on about the old days. Once they were done, Lexi aired out Drea's car the best way she could. She knew her sister was going to be pissed at her about smoking in her shit, but she would get over it eventually. When Aunt Shirley headed back in the house, Lexi went back over to Drea's to chill with her and get some perfume to cover up the weed smell. Lexi looked down at her phone to check out the time, she was ready to eat now that she was high as giraffe's pussy.

Chapter 27

Alyssa woke up early the next morning and got ready to pick Corey up from the airport. After she was dressed in pair of Ugg boots, a hoodie, and a pair of cut up jeans, she went to the study to ask her father could she borrow the keys to his Cadillac CTS. He informed her that he was about to head to the church and he would drive his truck, but if she got a scratch on his car, that he was going to put a scratch on her. Alyssa nodded her head in understanding before snatching the keys out his hands and rushing out the door. She unlocked the doors to the car, jumped behind the wheel, brought the car to life, and pulled off.

She arrived at the airport minutes later and drove to the arriving flights terminal. Alyssa parked in the loading zone with her flashers on and waited for Corey. Ten minutes later, she looked up just in time to see Corey walking through the sliding doors. Her mouth dropped at the sight of him. Corey was fly as fuck in his dark denim True Religion jeans, white True Religion hoodie with a fresh pair of wheat colored Timberland boots. His hair was freshly cut and needless to say, Corey was looking like a whole snack. Alyssa hadn't seen him in street clothes in a minute. He always wore suits and ties when he went to work. So, for her to see him dressed down made her pussy throb. She got herself together and unlocked the doors for him to get in. When he got in, they locked eyes for a few seconds before Corey broke the silence.

"You just gonna stare at a nigga or are you gonna give me some love?" he said with extended arms.

Alyssa damn near leaped into his lap as she hugged him tightly and kissed him passionately. She hadn't seen her fiancé in a week and she missed him so much.

“I can tell you missed a nigga,” he chuckled.

“You know I did,” Alyssa smiled.

“Look, before we go to ya parents’ house, I think we got some things we need to discuss.”

“Okay,” she answered dryly as she slid back into the driver seat.

“How about we go to IHOP?”

Alyssa didn’t answer. She turned the flashers off and pulled off into traffic. The radio drowned out the silence in the car, but Alyssa was wrapped up in her own thoughts. She knew what Corey wanted to talk about, which was a conversation she really didn’t want to have, but being as though he showed up after a week of no communication, she figured she’d play nice because she didn’t want him to leave. They arrived at IHOP minutes later and she parked in the first spot she saw. Corey helped her out the car and they walked arm and arm inside. They were seated immediately and when the hostess was gone, Corey jumped into the conversation.

“Look Alyssa, I’ve been doin’ a lot of thinkin’ about the situation at hand and I got over the fact that you’re an FBI agent because that shit’s actually a turn on and could maybe come in handy in the future. The real problem I have is the fact that you kept that shit from me. When you leave me in the dark, it makes me question you and look at you sideways like you’re keepin’ other shit from me. So, if there is anythin’ else that you’ve been keepin’ from me, you need to tell me now. Includin’ whatever beef you got with ya sisters and parents.”

Alyssa bit the inside of her jaw a few times before taking a deep breath.

"First, I want to apologize for not telling you about my new job, but to be honest with you, bae; I didn't tell anybody. Not even my folks. The only one that knows is Anastasia and that's only because I wanted some information out of her," she admitted.

"Damn. I thought you told everyone, but me."

She shook her head no. The waitress came over to their table, Corey gave their food and drink order, then she took off.

"So, let me ask you this? Who knows about me besides Anastasia?"

"Nobody." She lowered her head.

"Why are you keepin' shit from your family? If anythin', I thought ya other two sisters would know what's goin' on in ya life. Like, what the fuck is up?" he asked with confusion.

"What you mean?"

"Why the hell are you secretive to people that love and care about you? Since I've known you, you never talked about your family that much and the only reason you really came home is because ya oldest sister made you. If she wouldn't have called, you wouldn't have come home for the holidays, would you?"

"No, I wouldn't have. I'm not going to sit here and say that my life was fucked up because it wasn't, but the reason I don't share the important things that's going on in my life with my family is because I feel like my accomplishments don't mean shit to my parents and as far as my oldest sister, Andrea, and my baby sister, Alexis, all they care about are each other and our parents. They ask me all the time what's going on with me, but I don't tell them shit because they're frauds. They're asking to be fuckin nosey. They don't give a damn about what's going on with me," she expressed with anger. "That's why me and Anastasia are so close. Andrea is a daddy's girl. Alexis is a mama's girl and the middle children basically went unnoticed. That's why we moved away from here. I didn't want to constantly be in my sister's shadow. In New York, I don't have to compete with anyone, I have a great career and I have a man that loves me. My parents are going to love the fact that I'm engaged. That's all they want is for us to get married and have kids." She rolled her eyes.

"Damn, bae. I didn't know shit was like that with ya fam. I know you said that they don't know about me, but I'm sure someone spotted that rock on ya finger." He kissed her ring finger.

"Yeah. Andrea, the lawyer, did. After breakfast yesterday, she came up to my room and said some slick shit to me talking about your fiancé dumped you and now he's not answering your calls. I snapped on her ass a little bit, but apologized. I'm not trying to fight with my sisters, but I got a feeling that's not going to last for long."

"Yeah, that was a shady ass comment," he chuckled.

"Just be prepared for anything today, baby."

Their food came and they chowed down on French toast, sausage, and cheese eggs as Alyssa continued to fill him in about her family. Alyssa thought that the conversation they were going to have was mainly going to be about her job. She wasn't prepared to talk about her issues with her family and why she was closed off from them, but she felt that the conversation brought them closer in a way.

When they were finished, Corey paid the bill before leaving out of the restaurant. They hopped in the Caddy and Alyssa crunk up the car and drove home. She pointed out her favorite places and the schools she went to along the way. It felt good to share parts of her childhood with him. Alyssa parked the car back in its original spot and observed it to make sure it was scratch free because Daddy didn't play about his car. They walked inside, heading straight to the kitchen where all the chatter was. When they entered the kitchen, her mom smiled at the sight of them.

"Good Morning, Alyssa. I was wondering where you went off to" Victoria stood to hug her.

"Good morning, mom. I went to pick my friend up from the airport." She gave Corey a look letting him know to just go with it.

"Mommy, Daddy. This is my friend, Corey. Corey, these are my parents, Victoria and Abraham Holiday." She smiled.

"It's nice to meet you, young man." Victoria hugged him. "You must be somebody special. Alyssa don't visit us often and for her to invite you to dinner means something." She smiled.

"Mom!" Alyssa said through gritted teeth.

"What chile? It ain't like I'm lying," Victoria dismissed her with a hand wave.

"It's nice to meet you, Corey," Abraham greeted him with a handshake. "You look familiar, son. Like I seen you somewhere before."

"You probably seen him on TV, Daddy. He's a sports commentator," Alyssa bragged.

"ESPN, right?"

"Yes, sir," Corey chuckled.

"I like you already. Come on and let's talk in the living room. Alyssa, stay here and help your mother."

"Yes, Dad."

"I'm gonna kick ya ass for introducin' me as your fuckin' friend, Alyssa." Corey whispered in her ear.

"I'm sorry, baby. I panicked." Corey walked off joining and her father in the living room.

"Alyssa, baby, can you go next door and check on Andrea? I've been calling that chile all morning and she hasn't answered," Victoria spoke with concern.

"Okay, mom."

Alyssa did as she was told and went next door to her sister's house. Without knocking, she walked inside and was about to call for Andrea, but when she heard voices coming from the back near Drea's room, she decided not to. Closing the front door behind her, she quietly walked towards the back and listened to the conversation that was going on between Andrea, Alexis, and an unknown woman from behind the bathroom door. The conversation made Alyssa's mouth drop.

"Oh my God, Andrea is pregnant," she whispered to herself.

After hearing every detail of the conversation, the bathroom door opened and Andrea bumped into Alyssa on her way out. It took everything in her not to reveal what she just heard, but Alyssa figured she'd use the information to her advantage. She couldn't wait to get back to the house to tell Anastasia that their perfect sister and the apple of dad's eye, was having an illegitimate baby.

Chapter 28

Andrea laid in the bed all morning feeling like shit. Lexi had come by earlier that morning and let herself in with the spare key that was hidden outside and told her to cover for her if anyone asked where she stayed the night before. Of course, Andrea would cover for her little sister and would normally get the tea from her, but she didn't feel like it at the moment. Andrea rolled over and grabbed her phone from the nightstand and noticed that it was already after one o'clock. Since her phone was on silent, she didn't hear it ring, but noticed several missed calls and text messages.

Since Hannah was the last one to call, Drea hit her name and dialed her back. She didn't realize that it was a FaceTime call until she heard the sound. Hannah must have had the phone right in her hand because she answered right away.

"Bitch, I know YOU ain't still in the bed," Hannah gasped. "What the hell wrong wit you?" she continued.

It was very unlike Andrea to still be in bed at that hour, so she understood why her friend was alarmed.

"Girl… I been throwing up and shit. I don't know what's been wrong wit me, but I'm bout to get up," Drea told her girl.

"Throwing up? You never get sick. You pregnant?" Hannah asked.

It was at that exact moment that Drea realized that her cycle hadn't come on. She paused Hannah and clicked on the iPeriod app that she had installed on her phone. That app told your ovulating days and period days for twelve months out and it even went back a year. Drea's cycle was always like clockwork, and she saw that she was actually a week late. The shit hadn't even crossed her mind because she hadn't been having sex.

"New York," she mumbled.

"Oh, my gawwddd… we bout to have a baby," Hannah exclaimed, but Drea ignored her.

She looked back at the dates from a few weeks ago and noticed that she was indeed ovulating.

"Ain't no fuckin way," she sighed.

"I'm on my way," Hannah said, but Drea barely heard her.

She sat there in disbelief at the possibility that she could actually be pregnant by a man that she had a one night stand with. Andrea couldn't believe it. There was no way that she up and got pregnant on one night of fun. She decided that it must have just been stress that had her cycle late. Drea stood up and went to the bathroom to handle her hygiene. After she brushed her teeth, she got in the shower and allowed the hot water to cascade down her body. Her showerhead was set on jet stream and it felt like a massage to her suddenly stressed body. Andrea stayed in the shower so long that the water began to turn lukewarm, so she washed and rinsed off a couple of times, then finally got out.

Andrea dried off and wrapped her towel around her. She made her way to the kitchen and was thankful that she had some cans of ginger ale. After eating a few saltine crackers, she drank half the can and surprisingly, felt a little better. Andrea headed to her room, so that she could start getting dressed and head next door. She laid a pair of distressed Rock Revival jeans and an orange cardigan on the bed, then grabbed one of the pair of boots she had gotten from Belk the Saturday before. Drea wondered why people always got so dressed up for thanksgiving just to sit around the house and eat, but who was she to change the tradition. She slid her jeans and a white cami on, then heard a knock at the door.

Andrea made her way to the front and when she opened the door, she stood face to face with her best friend. Her eyes landed on a Walmart bag and she already knew what was inside.

"Girl, why you waste your money on some pregnancy tests?" Drea quizzed as she let Hannah inside.

"Wellll, that's to be determined and I know how your stubborn ass is, sooo I bought several," Hannah replied.

"Ain't no way I'm pregnant!" Drea fussed.

"Did you fuck or was that story all made up?" Hannah cocked her head to the side and Andrea gave her an evil glare. "My point exactly. If you fucked, then there's always a possibility," Hannah waved her off.

Andrea flipped her friend off and headed back to her room so she could finish getting dressed for the day. She took her bonnet off and brushed her hair. The hair that she had installed had been done three weeks ago, but if you looked at her you would have sworn that she had just gotten up out of the chair. After applying a small amount of edge control, she was good to go.

"Bitch, if you don't get your ass in the bathroom and take these tests!" Hannah demanded.

Andrea snatched the bag from her friend, who had laid across her bed, and went into the bathroom. She closed the door and looked into the bag and shook her head.

"Why the fuck you buy eight damn tests?" she hollered to Hannah's ass.

"Because I know yo ass gon say the first seven are wrong," Hannah yelled back.

She opened the door and went to the kitchen to get a plastic cup with Hannah watching her every move. Drea figured it made more sense to just urinate in the cup, so that she could take multiple tests instead of trying to piss on each stick. Once she made it back to the bathroom, she took two of the tests and waited for the results. It seemed like the plus sign instantly formed and Andrea's heart sank to her stomach.

"Drea!! It don't take that damn long!" Hannah exclaimed, then burst into the bathroom.

"Oh my God… you're really pregnant, bitch! Woowww!" Hannah stated.

"I gotta take two more… those can't be right!" Drea said, then dipped two of the other test into the cup.

Two pink lines popped up and she panicked.

"You wanna go ahead and do the other four and get them outta the way," Hannah quizzed, then took it upon herself to administer the other tests.

Sure enough, they all gave positive results and Drea slid down the wall and landed on the floor.

"My parents are gonna kill me!" she sighed.

"Girl… you grown. They'll be alright," Hannah tried to convince her.

"You don't even believe that… it was mess up the image of the church. And I'm not married," Drea stressed as she ran her hands through her hair.

"Andrea Holiday… it's not gonna kill them. You're grown and they'll be alright shit!"

"You just don't understand, Hannah," Drea sighed.

"What the hell y'all doin in here? Biiitttcchhhh you pregnant?" Lexi busted in the bathroom and said, after her eyes locked in on all of the pregnancy test and her sister sitting on the floor in tears.

"As you can see, she's in denial," Hannah pointed out.

"Shiiidddd I would be too. And she's daddy's favorite, too. He gon have a heart attack," Lexi expressed.

"Well, at least we know why you been sick. Now, get up because everybody looking for yo ass. I just came back from making a store run. We'll figure all this shit out," Lexi pulled her sister up from the floor.

It took about thirty minutes, but Andrea finally got herself together, with the help of her sister and friend. Thankfully the nausea was gone and she hoped that she could get through dinner without getting sick and enjoy the day with her family.

"You know you can't drink while you pregnant, right?" Hannah stated more than asked.

"Her ass been throwing back since yesterday… damn I hope you didn't fuck up my niece or nephew… it's probably both though," Lexi pondered.

Andrea shot them both a mean mug, then stopped in her tracks.

"Lexi is yo ass high?"

"You got some perfume? That's what the fuck I came over here for!"

Andrea pointed to her stash, then walked out of the room. She damn near bumped into Alyssa when she walked out of her room.

"Damn Lyssa… how long you been standing there?" Drea quizzed.

"I just walked up, Drea. I was coming to see what y'all was doing over here," Alyssa rolled her eyes.

"Her ass lying," Lexi mumbled.

They made their way out after Andrea grabbed her phone. She asked Hannah if she wanted to stay for dinner, but Hannah told her that she was about to head to her in-law's. Drea promised to call her later, then she headed to her parent's where she already knew the drama was waiting. She knew that Alyssa had to hear them talking, so she told herself to play nice, so that she wouldn't bust her out in front of everyone. When she walked in, she heard Aunt Shirley's mouth coming from the kitchen.

"Oh lord," Drea mumbled.

She made her way towards where all of the chatter was coming from.

"Drea, baby, you okay?" her mom asked when she made it in.

"Yes ma'am… I feel so much better now."

"What's wrong witcha, suga? You done finally had sex and got pregnant?" Aunt Shirley chimed in.

"Shirley… you just won't stop will you? Drea knows not to get pregnant before marriage," Mrs. Holiday mused.

"She sure does… my baby wouldn't do anything like that, but when her and Joseph tie the knot, she can have as many babies as she wants to," Mr. Holiday walked in and offered.

Andrea felt her anger level going from zero to one hundred just that fast and she hadn't even been in the house a full two minutes. She looked up and saw Anastasia and Alyssa whispering, but when Alyssa saw her looking, she turned her back to her. Andrea knew that arguing with her parents wasn't going to end well, so she bit her tongue and went and got the macaroni and cheese and chicken spaghetti out of the refrigerator that she made the day before and put it in the oven. She was happy when her mom left the kitchen as well as her dad.

"Y'all girls gon let them parents of y'all run y'all stone crazy. They asses ain't innocent as y'all think… better live y'all lives with no regrets like me," Aunt Shirley grumbled. "Let me liven this shit up anyway," Aunt Shirley continued and made her way to the stereo system in the living room that probably hadn't been on in years. The song that came on was *Ain't Gonna Bump No More* by Joe Tex.

"Aayyeee… this used to be my shit. *Three years ago, I was at a disco. Man, I wanted to bump, I was rarin' to go… and this big fat woman, bumped into me on the floor… she was rarin' to go, that chick was rarin' to go… man she did a dip, almost broke my hip."*

Aunt Shirley made her way back to kitchen singing and dancing, and just like that, everyone joined in with her. Everyone was surprised when Victoria did a dip.

"Look at my sister… she ain't always been a sour puss!" She didn't even get mad, she just laughed along with the family.

Everyone finished up with the dishes they prepared a little after two and they decided to go ahead and set the table since Mr. Holiday was back. Once they were done, everyone took their seats with smiles on their faces. Abraham prepared himself to say grace.

"Dear Lord, today we give thanks for our many blessings. We pray for those in need, lonely, and ill. Thanksgiving is a time of celebration and we are thankful to have our whole family under one roof on this day. Bless everyone to put their selfish ways aside and know when to listen to…."

Andrea loved her dad to death, but she tuned him out when he got to that part. Honestly, she was just ready to eat since she felt good and the aroma of the food had her stomach growling.

"Amen Abraham, damn… you gon preach Sunday!" Shirley cut him off and caused everyone to laugh under their breaths except Mr. and Mrs. Holiday.

"Before we eat, let's go around the table and everyone tell one thing that they are thankful for," Mrs. Holiday smiled and everyone sighed.

"Okay, I'll get mine outta the way… I'm thankful for mommy," Lexi beamed.

"Suck up," Stasia mumbled from across the table.

"I'm thankful to have everyone home," Drea said since she was sitting beside Lexi. She saw both Alyssa and Anastasia roll their eyes and since Alyssa was directly across from her, she kicked her.

"Ouch!"

"I'm thankful for all the laughs I'm bout to get from y'all fake asses," Shirley laughed.

"I'm thankful for God, for without him we wouldn't be here," Abraham bubbled.

"I'm thankful for my fiancé, Corey!" Alyssa exclaimed and held up her ring.

"Well praise God… two down, two to go… almost one," Abraham added while everyone congratulated Alyssa.

"Why you just getting here today though, Corey?" Shirley asked.

"You don't have to answer that… he's here now and that's all that matters," Alyssa rolled her eyes.

"I'm thankful to meet such a wonderful family," Corey spoke.

"I'm thankful that Jesus is gonna turn some water into wine in just a min," Anastasia proclaimed.

"Right on!" Shirley chimed in.

"All you do is drink," Richard shook his head.

"Gotta drink to deal with you," Anastasia mumbled low, but Drea heard her loud and clear and apparently, Aunt Shirley did, too; since she made the comment that there must be trouble in paradise.

"I'm thankful to have everyone here… having all of my babies under one roof is priceless… now let's eat."

Andrea put dressing, chicken spaghetti, fried chicken, and potato salad on one plate. When she grabbed another plate to get some greens, the doorbell rang, and since she was the closest to the door, she got up to answer it. When she opened the door, Andrea wondered if her sister was expecting company.

Chapter 29

Lexi's face was buried inside her phone when she heard the doorbell ring. She thought to herself that maybe Zyree took her up on her offer after all, but her thoughts were confirmed wrong when she heard her family say, "Breeeeee!" in unison. Lexi's eyes slowly raised from her phone just in time to see her best friend/lover walking into the dining room area with a huge smile on her face.

"Heyyyy Bre, we weren't expecting you, but have a seat." Lexi's father said, standing to his feet, greeting Bre.

"It's always a pleasure having you," Mrs. Holiday followed up saying behind her husband.

"Now, wait one damn minute, I ain't get that type of welcome," Aunt Shirley fumed, causing Alyssa's boyfriend Corey to laugh.

Bre went around the table speaking to everyone while purposely skipping Lexi. It was then that Lexi knew that she was on some good bullshit and to prepare herself.

"So Bre, how's school going for you?" Drea asked, handing Bre a dish so she could start making her plate.

"School is going great. I'm looking forward to graduation," Bre spoke while piling turkey, dressing, and macaroni and cheese on her plate.

"Child, you and Lexi sound alike," Mrs. Holiday giggled.

"But, I bet you not breaking your mother's heart by staying away in Atlanta after graduation, are you?" Victoria continued, piercing her eyes at Lexi.

Lexi caught the shade, but instead of acknowledging it, she grabbed her glass to take a sip of her Pepsi.

"Well, Mrs. Holiday, I am actually staying in Atlanta. My girlfriend decided to stay, so I'm staying as well," Bre announced.

Lexi spit out the soda in her mouth as she listened to Bre story about having a girlfriend.

"Uggghhh Lexi, watch what you doing," Drea said, wiping the soda off of her shirt.

"I'm sorry," she apologized while she cut her eyes at Bre.

"Ok wait, so we just gon' sit here and act like this child ain't just admit to having a girlfriend?" Aunt Shirley said, looking around the table at everyone.

"Auntie, it's 2017, you do know gay marriages are legal or are you still stuck in the 60s?" Stasia said, causing her sidekick Lyssa to laugh.

"I know what year it is, but I'm surprised you know about marriages since yours all fucked up," Aunt Shirley shot back, leaving everyone at the table with their mouths wide open.

Lexi was glad that their bickering was taking the spotlight off of Bre, but she was pissed off that she said what she said. Lexi wondered who spilled the beans about her being in Mississippi instead of New York.

"Ok ok ok Shirley, watch your mouth," Abraham warned, pointing his fork in her direction.

"Oh Abraham, shut the hell up. You think that being gay is a sin," Aunt Shirley stated.

"It's in the bible, Shirley. No offense to you, Bre," Mrs. Holiday said, taking up for her husband.

"Victoria be quiet, I know all your secrets from back in the days, so THY SHALL NOT speak about sin," Shirley said, imitating Mr. Holiday's voice.

"Oh my God, ya'll, chill. Let's enjoy this food that's before us," Alyssa said, defusing the situation for the time being.

For a few minutes, there was silence while everyone fed their faces. Lexi prayed to God that the day went as smooth as possible. She wanted to eat and get Bre the fuck out of her parents' house before she said some shit that would result in her getting her ass beat. Chatter began amongst Lexi's parents and her sisters, but she tuned them out. Her mind was everywhere at this moment and for the first time ever, she thought that Bre may actually be crazy enough to tell everyone what was going on between them.

Buzz... Buzz… Buzz... Buzz…

Lexi's phone vibrated on the table several times in a row, indicating that someone was texting her. When she finally looked up from her plate, she noticed Bre smiling at her with a sinister grin. Lexi rolled her eyes before grabbing her phone off the table right after it vibrated again.

"Someone thirsty to talk to you," Anastasia said as she placed more greens on Kyler's plate.

Lexi gave off a fake smile before opening the six unread text messages, all of them from J.R.

J.R.: Wyd

J.R.: When you coming home?

J.R.: Shorty, I think I miss you.

J.R.: You got me texting yo ass like a lame.

J.R.: lol aight I'm done

The fake smile that she gave off a few seconds ago, turned into a real one as she read those messages.

"Well dang, who got you cheesing like that?" Alyssa asked, but before Lexi could reply, Drea yelled out J.R.'s name.

Hearing his name alone caused butterflies to form in her stomach. At first, Lexi thought that she just liked his swag, but as the days went by, she was coming to terms with the fact that she was falling for him.

"And who is J.R.?" Mr. Holiday quizzed.

"He's my friend daddy," Lexi replied, before texting him back and placing her phone back on the table.

"Friend my as--- I mean butt…. J.R. got Baby Holiday nose wide opened," Drea teased.

"Shut up," Lexi snickered, elbowing her oldest sister.

"Well, when are we going to meet this friend?" their mother asked.

"I don't know mommy… I gotta see how it goes," Lexi blushed.

"Well, I can't wait to meet the man that has my baby sis looking all vibrant," Drea beamed, but Lexi heard Bre mumbling.

"Maybe we can meet him soon… what does he do?" Abraham chimed in.

"Oh, you really wanna know what he does?" Bre spoke up and Lexi stared at her, but she wouldn't make eye contact.

She knew that Bre didn't know anything about J.R., so there was no telling what was about to come outta her mouth.

"Bre, are you okay?" Drea quizzed with her head cocked to the side.

"No… I'm not okay. Lexi blew me to the side for this J.R. dude that got her stripping at blue flame.

Before Lexi could stop herself, she stood up and reached across the table and went after Bre, but Drea pulled her back.

"Stripping?" Lyssa and Stasia yelled in unison.

"And what the hell she mean by blew her to the side?" Aunt Shirley added.

"Yeah… y'all precious baby girl and sister is the top stripper at Blue Flame and we've been sleeping together for the past few years until this J.R. nigga popped into the picture!"

"You trifling bitch!" Lexi fumed as she tried to get away from Drea, all to no avail.

"Thanks for dinner, but I'm gonna leave now," Bre said and made her exit.

Lexi heard Alyssa and Anastasia mumbling and snickering, then she turned on them.

"What the fuck y'all snickering about?"

"Alexis Holiday!" Victoria shrieked.

"That's why Lexi my favorite!!" Aunt Shirley cheered.

"Shirley! Stop it… is what she said true, Alexis?" Abraham boomed.

Instead of answering out loud, Lexi fell back into her seat and nodded her head. She couldn't believe that Bre had really just aired her business out in front of her entire family. The thoughts she had running through her head for the next time she laid eyes on her weren't good at all. Her parents were talking, but Lexi tuned them out. She didn't mean to be disrespectful, but she couldn't process the shit that had just happened. She needed a blunt, and she needed one bad. When she stood to leave, her dad's voice made her stop in her tracks, so she had no choice, but to sit down and listen to what he had to say.

Chapter 30

After all of the drama at dinner the night before, the last thing Anastasia expected was for her family to still want to finish out the weekend. Of course, she didn't mind because for once she wasn't the one being judged. Anastasia felt bad that her baby sister had resorted to such measures to get money, but even worse that she was fucking the girl she had grown up being best friends with. That still wouldn't stop her from throwing jabs every chance she got though. Damn near everything Alexis said she found a way to comment about her being a stripper or being an undercover dyke. Of course, most of the time Andrea intervened, but that didn't stop Anastasia. She had a bone to pick with both of her funny acting sisters, and as soon as the opportunity, she was going to bust Andrea out with the news that Alyssa had given her.

It was surprising that they'd even wanted to continue with their plans to go Black Friday shopping together, but somehow Andrea had managed to get them all to go. They pulled into Walmart's parking lot and Anastasia frowned. She'd already had to ride next to Aunt Shirley's drunk ass, but looking at the store she didn't think they would fair well. For one, the outside was trashed and it wasn't nearly that many people out there. Not that Anastasia wanted to be around a crowd of irritated Americans fighting over scraps, but she knew that if it was empty, then the store was most likely cleaned out. She'd told Andrea that they should have went the night before at 12 like everybody else, but she wasn't trying to hear that.

"What the hell, it ain't even nobody here," Andrea mumbled, looking around before stepping out of her car.

"I told you we should have went last night," Anastasia snipped with an eye roll.

"Shit, we need to leave Walmart anyway, and head to the mall!" Lexi exclaimed. "I know all they sales bussin; especially VS."

"What you tryna go there for, some work clothes?" Anastasia asked with a frown. Lexi looked her way in obvious frustration while Alyssa gave her a high five.

"First off bitch!" she started getting loud and Andrea came to the rescue once again.

"Come on, I been waitin' for yo lil hot ass! Let her go Drea!" Anastasia yelled while Alyssa grabbed her arm to stop her from getting any closer.

"I swear yo ass act like you still in high school, Stasia! Leave this damn girl alone cause we all know damn well you ain't perfect!" Andrea pointed a finger in her face stopping her from struggling against Lyssa. "And Lexi stop letting everything her bitter ass say get to you! You don't have to answer to nobody about what or who you do, especially her," she said, turning to face Lexi. With Drea right there, she calmed down quickly.

"You right big sis… I'm good," Lexi grumbled with her eyes cut in Anastasia's direction.

"That ain't right, Drea. You always taking her side about shit. If it would have been me, both ya'll asses would have been talkin' shit! You always on that favoritism shit I swear," Anastasia fumed, snatching out of Lyssa's hold.

"All ya'll bitches need to shut up! In the parking lot of Walmart ain't the place to be airing this shit out. We all know Alexis is a lil strippin' dyke now and we all know Anastasia ass bitter as hell cause she don't want Richard ole crusty ass! Now, leave that girl alone so we can go on in this store and I can see what deals they got on this liquor up in here!" Aunt Shirley snapped, getting in between them all as she fixed her wig on her head. Anastasia's face twisted up into a frown at her putting her business on front street, but she didn't say anything and neither did Lexi, even though her face held the same irritation. They both knew that there was no arguing with Shirley; especially, when she was drunk, and she had already filled her flask twice that morning. With a satisfied smirk, Andrea looped her arm through Lexi's and walked ahead of them all. Anastasia and Alyssa shared a look cause they already knew that they were up there talking shit about them.

"Come ya'll asses on! I don't know why ya'll so cliqued up and ya'll all siblings," Aunt Shirley continued to fuss, waving them ahead of her.

With a deep sigh, the two sisters entered the store with their Aunt behind them still going off. Anastasia grabbed a cart hoping that she could at least find something to get Kyler since she knew the early risers had already been all through there. She was glad that he had gone with his father instead of tagging along with them since they hadn't even been alone for an hour and had already gotten into an argument.

"Sis, you know I got yo back," Alyssa whispered to her, so that their Aunt Shirley wouldn't hear. She gave her a sympathetic look and patted her back as they maneuvered through the store to get to the electronic section.

"I know, boo; apparently, you're the only one."

"Stasia, you already know it's been like that. Drea gone always come to Lexi's defense and I'm gone always come to yours, it ain't right, but it's just how shit goes," Lyssa shrugged, grabbing a candle set off the shelf and throwing it in the cart.

"It's still fucked up," Anastasia noted and Alyssa merely nodded. She didn't know when things had turned into a tag team affair whenever the sisters were around each other, but she wasn't about to let this shit with Lexi die down. Like she'd said, if it would have been her who had a secret lesbian affair with her childhood friend and had been shaking her ass in somebody's club for dollars, all hell would have broken loose. She was tired of Lexi always getting off easy and Andrea always taking up for her right or wrong, so until she saw fit, she was gonna bring up the situation every chance she got.

At some point the girls lost their Aunt, but found their sisters in the electronics department. Still a little irritated about the whole argument, Stasia kept a small distance between them as she tried to find Kyler some headphones and games in all of the rubbish. Luckily, she was able to find a few games that were age appropriate and even a couple of movies despite the chaos that had taken place there that morning. She was even able to find Richard a camera and a cute digital picture frame to go in his office. Knowing him, he'd find something to complain about even though she didn't have to bring his ass shit.

"Oh, my God! Anastasia!" Stasia heard her name being called and turned around to see Lizz standing there with a cart and a huge grin. Surprised. she made her way over to her and exchanged air kisses and a hug.

"Hey girl! What you doin down this way?" she wanted to know.

Lizz had never mentioned having family down south and Jackson was the last place anybody would come for vacation, let alone Lizz's stuck up ass.

"Oh, you know the fellas had that damn conference out this way," Lizz chuckled a little bit and looked away.

"Oh duh," Stasia joined her and gave her arm a tap.

Of course, Harold would have to attend the same conference as Richard. They worked closely together and most times you wouldn't see one without the other. She was shocked that Lizz had decided to join him though. Usually, when Harold went out of town, she would leave with her lil boo until he returned, but it was still good to see her nevertheless.

"You here alone?"

"Aw hell yeah! You know Harold's old ass ain't tryna be out going to all these stores." She waved her off with another laugh.

"I know right. It would have been like pulling teeth to get Richard out here." Anastasia rolled her eyes. She could see Alexis and Andrea next to the cd's, but looking in their direction. Figuring that they were talking about her being rude for not introducing them, she sucked her teeth. "Come meet my sister's girl before they say I'm actin' funny."

"Uhh…I was actually about to leave," Lizz trailed off, turning away slightly. "I'll just catch you later."

"Don't be silly, it's only gone take a minute," Anastasia insisted, pulling her over to where her sisters stood. Alyssa made her way towards them at the same time and Stasia went ahead and introduced them all quickly.

"Guys this is my friend, Lizz, from New York, Lizz, these are my sisters Andrea, Alexis, and Alyssa," she said, pointing at each one as she named them. They all waved, but Anastasia noticed Lexi and Drea share a look after they gave her a dry ass hey.

"It's nice to meet you all, but ummm I was on my way out. Harold been blowing me up," she said, looking at her phone like it would ring any minute.

"Well okay, just hit me up. Me and Richard are gonna be here until Sunday night. We should get together before we go back," Stasia drawled, giving her a strange look. She didn't really understand the rush, when she knew that Lizz never did anything when or how Harold wanted.

"Alright, I will," she called over her shoulder as she walked away with her phone to her ear. When she turned back to her sisters, Drea and Lexi were watching Lizz's retreat, before Lexi shrugged and went back to browsing the cd's in her hand.

"Ya'll was just rude as hell," Anastasia tilted her head and looked over to her sisters with knitted brows. "Is that how strippers act when they meet new people?"

"Bitch, you ain't got but one more time to come for me-."

"And what's gone happen? Huh? Not shit!" Stasia damn near shouted lunging in her sister's direction. She was yanked back before she could get too close, while Drea put an arm up to hold Lexi back.

"Ughhhhhh! I swear you talk so much fuckin' shit bitch and yo shit ain't nowhere near as perfect as you think!" Lexi shouted trying to get around Drea.

"Don't do this shit here, Alexis!" Andrea hissed, struggling with Lexi.

"So, what hoe? We all know that I ain't happy with Richard, sooooo what? At least I got a man and ain't out here dancing for dollars and getting' fucked with a strap on!"

"We don't use a strap you dumb ass hoe! I ride that hoe face just like that bitch that just left rides Richard's!" Lexi snapped, clapping her hands after each word. Shocked, Anastasia stopped fighting against Alyssa and blinked confused.

"What the fuck you talkin' bout, Lexi?" She wanted to know, now trying to get around Andrea who was looking defeated.

"I'm sayin that your "husband" been fuckin' yo so-called friend dummy! That's what she doin' out here!"

"I told you not to bring that shit up here, Lexi, damn!" Andrea sighed loudly, throwing her head back.

"Oh, so you knew about this shit too, Drea? And ya'll bitches wasn't gone say shit?" Anastasia let out a bitter laugh and shook off Lyssa as she tried to wrap her arms around her shoulders.

"I swear I just found out when ole girl walked up," Drea turned to face her with both hands up in defense.

"Right and ya'll lettin' me sit here and keke with this hoe and didn't say shit?" she asked with a trembling voice. "Ya'll want to see me hurt that bad, huh?"

"Oh, bitch please! First of all, you don't even want that nigga, and secondly, you been throwing shots at me like a muthafucka, now you want to sit and act like you soooo hurt! Miss me with that shit. Shouldn't have allowed your husband to stay at a fuckin hotel without you. That's where I saw em at," Lexi smacked her lips and waved Stasia off.

"That shit still ain't cool, Lexi, and you know it! Real shit, ya'll should have said somethin' and we all was sposed to get in that hoe ass regardless," Alyssa finally spoke and for the first time, Stasia thought about the fact that Lizz's hoe ass might possibly still be there.

Without saying a word, she took off running back towards the front of the store in search of that pale bitch. She scanned the lines and saw that she wasn't at any of the registers before rushing out the automatic doors with Alyssa calling her back.

"Ahhhh!" she yelled loudly as she looked through the lot for any sign of that bitch. Anastasia knew she was long gone, but she wouldn't stop walking through the parking lot.

"Anastasia, calm down!" Alyssa yelled, grabbing ahold of her arm so that she couldn't continue to walk up on cars.

"Calm down? You want me to calm down when this lame ass nigga been fuckin' my so-called friend behind my back?"

"Yes Stasia! Be real with yourself, you don't even really care! This is a way for you to get out of your marriage easy! Can't you see that!" she pleaded, but Anastasia wasn't trying to hear any of that shit. Regardless of if she wanted to be with Richard or not, she was still pissed that he had the audacity to fuck someone else, let alone someone she called a friend. Sure, she had her someone on the side, but at least he didn't know the person. He had that bitch in her face day in and day out like it was okay.

"You think I give a fuck! We all know this shit wasn't about love!" Anastasia shouted with her arms spread. "This shit is about respect! Off GP that bitch was off limits!" she didn't care that there were people standing there watching her act a fool, she didn't care about anything at that moment, but getting at that bitch for disrespecting her and fucking Richard up.

"Stasia, calm yo ass down out here givin these white folks a show!" Aunt Shirley came out of nowhere shuffling across the parking lot with a bag in one hand and her flask in the other. "Gone on about ya'll business! Out here being nosey and shit like ya'll don't be fuckin ya'll cousins, brothers and sisters! Ole inbred asses!" she growled, waving off the group of bystanders that were standing there. They all walked off slowly knowing that they didn't want any problems with the loud mouth lady in the blue dress.

"Naw, right now ain't the time, Aunt Shirley!"

"You think I give a damn about what time it is girl? You out here showin' yo natural black ass and for what?"

"Oh, you don't know! It seems my damn husband has been fuckin' my friend and nobody bothered to tell me!" she said, slapping a hand against her chest angrily.

"Aw girl please, anybody with half a damn brain can tell that Richard cheating on yo ass fool! You think that man don't know you ain't happy? I know yo ass ain't doing shit wifely, so of course he was gone find somebody to fulfill those needs! You feel that highly of yourself that you don't think he would want anybody but you?" Aunt Shirley asked, instantly shutting her up.

"I ain't tryna hear that shit right now, Aunty," Anastasia shook her head fighting the truth of her words.

"Oh, so you cursing me, now? Huh? Yo ass ain't that mad and you damn sure ain't too grown for me to whoop yo yellow ass!"

Anastasia was so mad that her vision was blurry and the last thing she wanted was to sit and listen to her Aunty go in on her when she wasn't the one in the wrong, well to their knowledge anyway. Where the fuck was she when Alexis had put her business out there inside of a damn Walmart? She blew a frustrated breath and closed her eyes as she tried to gather her thoughts.

> "Stasia, let's just get out of here," Alyssa suggested, wrapping her arms around her sister. "I already set up an Uber," she let her know as Anastasia fell into her embrace while she rubbed her back.

It didn't even take the Uber five minutes to get there, letting Anastasia know that her sister had been setting up the ride while she had her meltdown. Lyssa always knew what to do and when to do it and in that moment, she was happy to have at least one of her sisters in her corner. They both climbed inside of the awaiting car and Anastasia couldn't wait to get home, so that she could fuck Richard up. She watched her sisters come out of the store and meet their Aunt at the car before they pulled away.

Chapter 31

As soon as the car drove off, Anastasia was on her phone calling Richard's punk ass. He ignored her the first time, but picked up on the first ring the second time.

"Hello?" he answered and she could hear the hesitation in his voice because she never really called him for anything.

"Where the fuck you at Richard?"

"I'm at the house…. why?" he questioned, sounding nervous.

"Cause I just ran into yo lil hoe, Lizz, at Walmart nigga!" she snapped. "I'ma fuck you and her up, so stay yo ass right there!" she continued as the line went silent. Pulling the phone away from her ear, she realized that the nigga had hung up on her. "Oh no the fuck he didn't!"

"What?"

"That pussy ass nigga hung up on me!" Stasia vented furiously as she attempted to call him back. Of course, he kept sending her ass to voicemail, but that didn't stop her from calling.

"What did you call him for? You should have just popped up on his ass and started fuckin him up, now he know and he probably gone be gone by the time we get there," Lyssa commented rolling her eyes.

"Oh, he bouta catch this fade! It ain't nowhere he can run that I won't find his ass!" she couldn't believe that he had done something so low down.

How long had they been fucking around? When had it started? Was that hoe telling him her business? Did he know about D'Mani? Those were all the questions running through her mind as the car cruised back to her parent's house. She knew that they were both unhappy, and yeah, she might have felt like Richard wouldn't cheat on her, but a small part of her knew that something was going on. Her friend though? That was the last person she expected for him to have been having an affair with. Richard was just like Lizz's husband, Harold, only younger. What in the hell had made her want to talk to the black version of her husband? The way that she'd talked about him had made it seem as if he was laid back and down to earth, the total opposite of Richard. Anastasia wondered if maybe he had just been putting on a show for her benefit this whole time and really wasn't as uptight as he made himself out to be.

"I'm still stuck on the fact that them hoe ass sisters of ours didn't say shit!" Alyssa vented.

"Like you said, Drea and Lexi always gone have each other backs and we gone do the same," Stasia said shaking her head.

She had a problem with her sisters too for keeping some information like that away from her. It seemed like they had planned on not telling her and probably laughing about it behind her back.

"If that's how you see it," Alyssa mumbled with an eye roll as the car pulled up to the house. Anastasia noticed that Richard's rental wasn't parked out front, but that didn't stop her from jumping out of the car and speed walking into the house ready to get into Richard's ass.

She stormed through the house and looked for him getting pissed off as she came up empty. She should have known his ass was gone try and leave when she mentioned Lizz's hoe ass. It would have been smarter to have done what Lyssa had said and just popped up on his ass. She ran back down the stairs to see her standing in the living room as Drea, Lexi, and Aunt Shirley all filed into the front door.

"Where the hell that nigga at!" Aunt Shirley asked, looking around the living room.

"He's gone already," Alyssa explained, glancing in her direction. They all stepped further inside of the house and Anastasia noticed that both of her sisters had sour looks on their faces.

"You must have called him before you got here?" Andrea observed.

"Why do you even care, bitch? Yo ass wasn't worried about me earlier," Anastasia watched as Drea closed her eyes and took a deep breath like she was getting on her nerves.

"Anastasia, what you ain't gone do is act like it's my fault yo husband was fuckin yo friend! You know damn well if we would have told you, you wouldn't have believed shit we said, so cut it the fuck out!" Andrea called her out.

"Preach!" Alexis spoke up from on the side of her.

"That's not true!" Anastasia tried to lie.

She knew that if they would have brought that information to her before they had run into Lizz, she would have never believed it. It wasn't like they had the best relationship, so there would have been no reason for her to believe that they were telling her the truth.

"Listen, I'm not about to argue with you, Stasia. You know what I'm saying is true. Regardless of what you may think of us though, we do love you and we weren't trying to keep it away from you to hurt you. I wanted to figure out the best way to approach the situation, because at Walmart this morning wasn't the time or place."

"Listen to yo damn sister for once and stop being so fuckin stubborn!" Aunt Shirley scolded from her spot on the couch.

"Ya'll need to put ya'll differences aside for the time being and go whoop Richard's ass together!" she exclaimed.

The sister's all looked around, each considering what their Aunt was saying. They all knew that even though they'd had their issues in the past they always put them aside to band together when the situation called for it. Those moments were few and far between, but they had happened and now was one of those times.

Anastasia's phone vibrated in her hand and she unlocked the screen to see a text from Richard.

Richard: I left Kyler there with your mother and went back to the hotel. I don't have time to argue with you about your crazy assumptions, Ana.

Anastasia: Oh, you can text, but yo bitch ass can't answer the phone, huh?

She waited for a reply, but it never came and she knew he saw it because his read receipts were on. That nigga was really trying to turn this shit around on her like she was crazy or some shit. For as stuck up as Richard wa,s he was doing typical hood nigga shit and Anastasia was not standing for it.

"Uggghh I'ma fuck him up!" she shrieked loudl,y stopping the conversation that was going on around her.

"What?" Lyssa asked with her brows knitted together and everyone's eyes landed on Anastasia.

"That nigga just texted and said he left Kyler with mama and he's gone cause he ain't tryna argue with me about my crazy assumptions!"

"His ass know damn well," Alexis sucked her teeth.

"He think he slick! He know I don't know what hotel his ass is in."

"Well, I do and I know what room he in," Alexis let it be known with both hands on her hips. A hush fell over the room.

"Ya'll bitches tryna do a Holiday sister beat down or nah?"

"I'm with it," Andrea shrugged and began to tie back her hair.

"You already know I'm comin," Lyssa chimed in.

"Yessss, that's what I'm talkin' bout! Now, let's go!" Aunt Shirley exclaimed as she popped up from the couch.

Anastasia immediately started shaking her head no.

"Hell, naw, Aunty! You too old to be tryna fight anybody. You stay here," she said, causing their Aunt to smack her lips.

"Who you callin' old? I can twerp this booty and knock a hoe out just like ya'll can, shit!"

"First of all, it's twerk, Aunt Shirley," Andrea sighed and pinched the bridge of her nose while Lexi laughed.

"Shiiiit, I say we bring her," Lexi said with a wide grin.

"Ya'll wastin' all this time and I'm comin' no matter what! Now, let's go before that tight booty ass nigga of hers leave and I have to catch a flight!" Aunt Shirley snapped, walking past all of them and out of the front door. Alexis was the first one to follow behind her, then Andrea went out right after. Anastasia let out a heavy sigh and motioned for Alyssa to follow her, and they both filed out after their sisters, locking the door behind them.

When they pulled up at the Residence Inn thirty minutes later, Anastasia turned up her nose at the thought of them having been there fucking the whole time. Even though she had done her dirt somehow, she still felt betrayed by finding out that Richard was cheating. Maybe it was because it was a blow to her confidence. Anastasia never thought that he would cheat on her, especially not with someone she considered a friend. She real life was blind-sided by this whole thing and even worse, it had all come out in front of her sisters.

"Oh, he got this hoe in a nice lil hotel, huh? He a damn dummy, all real niggas know that you take yo side hoe to a cheap ass hotel; that's what they named for Hoe! Tell!" Aunt Shirley started going off as soon as Andrea put the car in park. She damn near knocked Anastasia down trying to get out.

"What room they in, Lexi?" Andrea asked their little sister as soon as they all were out of the car.

"I saw them go in room 308. That's on the third floor," she told them before heading inside without waiting.

They each walked past the front desk not worried about being stopped, but they could easily just say that Anastasia was trying to surprise her husband. Luckily, there was no one behind the desk when they came in, so they all filed inside of the elevator.

"Oooh, I can't wait to beat this nigga ass!" Lexi fumed, watching the numbers go up.

"Calm yo ass down, Lexi; this Stasia fight," Andrea said, causing Lexi to give her a crazy look.

"Now, you know Anastasia ass ain't gone want no parts in this for real…"

"Oh, naw this all me, ya'll," Anastasia cut her off just as the bell dinged and the doors slid open.

Alexis tried to beat her sisters off of the elevator, but Anastasia managed to get through the doors first. She stormed down the halls checking the numbers on each door until she found Richard's. With a raised hand, she prepared herself to knock on the door when Alyssa grabbed her arm to stop her.

"Bitch, if he see you at this door he ain't gone open it," she hissed in a whisper in case he could hear them on the other side of the door.

"Shit," Anastasia mumbled because she hadn't thought about that, but before they could come up with a plan, Aunt Shirley pushed her way through them and knocked on the door covering the peephole with a finger. They all looked at her in shock, not sure of what she was going to say.

"Naw, Aunt Shirley…" Andrea began, but Aunt Shirley waved her off and told her to shut her ass up. With a frown, she pursed her lips together and folded her arms.

"Who is it?" Rich's voice broke through the silence that followed and Aunt Shirley cleared her throat.

"Room service," she slurred in what was supposed to be a Spanish accent, but it came out sounding like she was a cartoon character. They all fought to hold in the laughter that threatened to come out from her attempt at disguising her voice.

"I didn't order anything from room service," he grumbled as he opened the door with his head down. As soon as there was enough space to fit through, Alexis threw a jab that landed right on his nose causing it to leak.

"What the fuck?"

"Yeah nigga! You thought you was gone get away with playin my sister, huh?" Alexis shouted, pushing her way inside the room as Richard tried to close the door on them. She landed another blow to his face knocking him on his ass and they all filed inside of the room.

"Bitch, I told you I wanted to hit his ass first!" Anastasia said, sucking her teeth. She grilled Lexi who now stood over Richard and shrugged with a smile.

"Shit, I was just warming him up for you."

"I'm going to call the police!" Richard cried from his spot on the floor with his hand over his nose.

"You ain't callin shit, bitch!" Lexi ranted and kicked in his direction.

"I knew his ass was a pussy!" Anastasia heard her Aunt say from behind her.

"Oh yes, the hell I am! Ana, why would you bring your sister's here to try and fight me?" he wanted to know.

"Shut up! You don't get to ask her no questions," Andrea who was standing behind him now spat and slapped him on the back of the head.

"Fuck him up, Stasia!"

Anastasia stepped closer to him and was now standing between his legs. She squatted in his face and slapped the cowboy shit out of him. She laughed at how he dramatically grabbed the side of his face and looked up at her in fear.

"You know you got some nerve to be cheating on me with that bitch, Lizz!" she said through clenched teeth. "All this time, I been trying to stick it out with you, and you go and do this!" She went to hit him again, but paused as he began to laugh.

"Really Anastasia? I got some nerve when you've been fucking a low life thug behind my back for how long?" he asked with a bitter laugh as her eyes widened in shock. "Oh, you didn't think I knew, huh?

"This ain't about her! This about your low-down ass. Shit, I'd be fuckin a thug too if I had to sleep next to yo boring ass every night!" Lexi scoffed from the side.

"Shit, ain't that the truth! He don't even look like he got good dick, hell! I ain't even got my glasses on and I can see that," Aunt Shirley chimed in and all eyes landed on her. Of course, she had her flask out and Anastasia shook her head at her Aunt who merely shrugged and took another sip.

"Anyway," Stasia dragged. "That's not the same thing, Richard! That was my friend! You introduced us!"

"Speakin of which, where that hoe at?" Alyssa questioned, looking around as if she would just appear out of nowhere.

"Hell yeah, that's what I wanna know!" Andrea added.

"Why are they even here, Ana, damn!"

"Bitch, don't question us! We here to beat yo ass!" Richard looked up at Lexi and rolled his eyes.

"You just showin yo ass cussin and bragging on fuckin that hoe to me, huh?" Anastasia tilted her head and gave him a sinister grin. She really didn't even know how she had put up with his shit all of this time for fear that D'Mani would play her out when her safety net had been doing it all along.

"Look Ana, I don't know what you want me to say. I'm confused on why you're even so upset when you don't even want to be with me. The only thing keeping us together is my son at this point and you know it," he tried to reason with her as he wiped the small trickle of blood from his lip. She couldn't even lie and say that she didn't understand his point, because what he was saying was true. There were no feelings there, but she still felt betrayed by him and the bitch that she had considered a friend. To top that off, she had wasted so much time pushing D'Mani away for him and she might have lost him forever when her own husband had been fucking around on her.

"Don't try and turn this shit around on her, nigga!" Lyssa said sucking her teeth. "Don't nobody got no sympathy for you."

"Where is she?" was all Stasia wanted to know at this point.

They had gotten their round with him and now, it was Lizz's turn. There was no way that she could allow that hoe to get off scott free, she was most definitely catching a fade. He shook his head and mumbled something under his breath that she couldn't make out.

"You think this shit is a game? Where that hoe at?" Alexis yelled and tried to get at him, but Andrea held her back.

"I honestly don't know and I wouldn't tell you anyway, fuckin' bitch!" he said with narrowed eyes.

"See, I was tryna save yo ass!" Andrea said and let Lexi go. As soon as she was free, she ran over and they all started kicking him as he wailed in pain. Even Aunt Shirley went over and threw in a few licks with her purse. They were all digging in his ass until a pounding at the door stopped them. Richard rolled around on the floor moaning in pain and Lyssa squatted in his face and slapped him.

"Shut up, bitch boy."

"Security! Open this door!" They all heard from the other side and their eyes widened in surprise.

"Oh, shit ya'll I'm on probation! I can't be goin back to jail!" Aunt Shirley whispered, taking a long gulp of her drink. She started mumbling to herself and they all looked at her like she was crazy.

"What is you doin?"

"Shit, I'm prayin'. God gotta come through!"

"Lawd Aunty, chill out. I got this," Alyssa sighed and stood up, straightening out her clothes before heading to the door.

"Wait bitch, don't open that!" Lexi hissed, but Lyssa waved her off and went to open the door.

Two beefy security guards stood on the other side with scowls on their faces. Thankfully they couldn't see Richard from where they stood, and Lexi stood right next to him and threatened to fuck him up if he made a sound.

"May I help you gentlemen?" Alyssa asked with a smile on her face. The two guys looked her over, then their eyes swept the room before coming back to her.

"Yes, we've been receiving calls about yelling and screams coming from this room." The biggest of the two said stepping closer, but she put a hand up to stop him.

"Sorry about that fellas," she said and pulled out her badge.

"I got a fugitive in here and he was putting up a little bit of a fight, but me and my associates have it under control."

The two men eyed her badge, then looked around the room again at all of the sisters since Aunt Shirley had moved behind the wall with Alexis and Richard. The one who spoke first nodded his head in understanding, then backed up a little. "FBI huh? How about you let me take you out sometime, cause I ain't never seen an agent that looked like you." He tried his luck at flirting and Anastasia immediately let out a sigh of relief. If he was trying to flirt with Alyssa that meant that they didn't see them as a threat.

"Sorry honey, but I'm engaged," she told him, flashing her ring. "But, the bureau appreciates your fast response." With that, she closed the door in his face. When she turned back around to face her sisters, Andrea was giving her a slow clap while Stasia and Lexi were laughing their asses off.

"Damn, that was close girl. I'm glad you had your badge on you," Drea said beaming.

"Nah, fuck all that! Bitch, you the jakes?" Aunt Shirley gasped.

"Yes, Aunt Shirley, I work for the FBI," Lyssa replied with an eye roll.

"That's some shit you need to disclose before I come around, girl; ain't no tellin' what I might have confessed to around yo ass," she fussed.

"Look, we done beat his ass and almost got caught, let's just go before anything else happen," Andrea suggested and they all agreed.

"Hell yeah, I made my point already," Lexi trilled and flipped her hair over her shoulder.

"Okay, but before we go." Alyssa stopped them and pulled her gun out of her purse pointing it in Richard's face.

"You are not to tell anyone about this, understood?" she coaxed and with his nose turned up, Richard nodded his understanding.

"Okay Richard, I'm giving you a chance here. I would hate for my nephew to lose his daddy because you made the dumb decision to lie to me." She stared him down for a few more seconds before popping up to her feet and tucking her gun away.

"Now, we can go ya'll." She shrugged while they all stared at her in surprise. Well, all except Lexi who had a wide grin on her face.

"Yo, that shit was gangsta as hell!" she gushed. "I gotta get me one of them lil bitches."

"Hell yeah, me, too!" Aunt Shirley added as they both walked past Richard and she smacked him upside the head with her purse. Shaking her head, Andrea followed them out with Alyssa right behind her.

Anastasia looked down at the man that she'd spent the last few years of her life with as he wiped at his nose since it wouldn't stop bleeding. With a shake of her head, she stepped around him.

"Good bye, Richard," she said with her head held high as she walked away.

"Oh, and I want a fucking divorce!" Were her last words as she slammed the door shut on him and their marriage.

Chapter 32

A knock on her bedroom door woke Alyssa up the next morning. She didn't know what time it was, but after the crazy evening she had endured with her sisters and Aunt, she wasn't ready to welcome the new day yet. Tossing the covers off her, she dragged herself out of bed and over to the door. She opened the door halfway and saw her dad standing on the other side.

"Good morning, sleepy head," he said with a chipper tone.

"Hey Dad! What's going on?" Alyssa asked in a groggy tone.

"I just came back from getting the Christmas tree and I need that fiancé of yours to help me bring the decorations out of the basement. So, hurry and get yourself together."

"What time is it?"

"Almost eleven. I woke your sisters up, too. So, don't think I'm just picking with you," he chuckled.

"Okay, Dad. We'll be down in a minute." She closed the door and grabbed her suitcase looking for something to wear. After picking out her outfit, Alyssa woke Corey up with a light shake.

"I'm up, Lyssa and I know your father wants me to help him bring the decorations up from the basement."

"Well, get your ass up and get ready." She hit him playfully in his head.

"I'm surprised you're still here. I thought you would've been on the first plane out of here after what happened a couple days ago."

"I ain't gonna lie. Ya family definitely got some issues, bae, but that's not enough to scare me away. Ya Aunt Shirley is crazy as fuck though," he chuckled.

"Who you telling?" She shook her head.

Alyssa watched as Corey got out of bed and threw on a tee shirt over his wife beater and a pair of pajama pants. It had been a while since she had some dick and wanted to fuck him badly, but she couldn't bring herself to fuck him in her parents' house. They shared a quick kiss before they walked out the room heading in different directions. Alyssa walked to the bathroom and handled her hygiene before getting dressed for the day.

A little while later, she walked downstairs where she found her dad, sisters, nephew, and Corey in the living sorting through decorations, while her mother and Aunt Shirley were cooking in the kitchen. Alyssa greeted all her sisters and nephew with hugs before helping with the decorations. For the first time since she arrived, Alyssa was at ease with spending time with her sisters. Whooping Richards' ass the night before seemed to bring them closer and for the first time since she arrived, the tension was gone. Alyssa couldn't recall when the relationship with her sisters became so strain, but it felt good to bond with them.

After they sorted through all the decorations, Alyssa and Andrea began decorating the living room while Alexis, Anastasia, and Kyler decorated the tree. Victoria and Aunt Shirley made everyone take a lunch break and as soon as they were finished, they went back to decorating and everyone gathered in the living room. The laughter, talking and joking added to the peaceful atmosphere as they finished decorating the house.

Around five that evening, Alexis and Anastasia went into the kitchen to help their mother warm up the leftover Thanksgiving food while everyone else hung out in the living room. Alyssa sat next to Corey on the couch and Aunt Shirley was sitting next to Alyssa with her flask in hand. Their dad sat comfortably in his favorite chair while Andrea was posted up in the doorway. Abraham was in control of the TV and when he turned to the news, they sat quietly and watched. A few minutes later, a story about an innocent young black man who they portrayed as a thug being gunned down by white cops in a case of mistaken identity caught everyone's attention. Aunt Shirley nudged Alyssa to get her attention and nodded her head in her fathers' direction. Alyssa saw how upset he was and before she could ask what was wrong, her father spoke.

"These freaking cops make me sick. They're always so quick to gun down the innocent. They don't care if they have their facts straight or not. All they care about is that they got another black man off the streets. Didn't help me to see this on the day of my brother's death anniversary," he fumed.

"Daddy, don't tell me you still have ill feelings towards that cop," Alyssa asked in disbelief.

"After they shot and killed my twin brother because of mistaken identity, you damn right I do! My brother was an upstanding citizen, not the thug they wanted him to be and think all blacks are!" he stared at her. "Cops don't give a damn about no one, except for their own kind. The officer that killed my brother didn't lose his badge or serve any jail time. Everyone in law enforcement are a bunch of pigs.

Including the black people that work in that field," he boomed.

Alyssa looked around the room and all eyes were on her except for her fathers'.

"I know that it must hurt dad, but you can't blame all law enforcement for the mistake one man made."

"Alyssa, you gonna just sit there and act like you don't know the pain it caused? How dare you… all cops can go to hell if you ask me!

"So, I guess I'm going to hell? Huh, Dad?"

"What?" he looked at her again.

"I'm an FBI agent, Daddy. So, that makes me a pig too? And it means I'm going to jail?"

Abraham stood to his feet and so did Alyssa. They met each other in the middle of the floor and stared at each other for a minute. Everyone had gathered into the living room, but the room was so quiet you could hear a mouse piss on cotton.

"Aww shit, now. This gonna be a good one right here! But wait… Lyssa you better remember I'm your aunt. I got warrants and shit, but you better stay the hell away from me!" Aunt Shirley cackled as she took a drink from her flask.

"Please tell me that you're joking, Alyssa," Abraham winced.

"No, I'm not. I've been an agent for a couple of months now."

"Well you need to call and tell them that you resigned," he demanded.

"I will do no such thing. I like what I do and I will not quit my job because of your ill feelings towards law enforcement. What happened to our uncle was unfortunate, but it happened years ago. You need to learn how to forgive and let it go, Dad."

"I will never forgive them for what they did to my brother," he boomed.

"Abraham, you're so full of shit. How the hell are you preachin' every Sunday and tellin' your congregation to be like Christ and you're doin' the complete opposite? Jesus forgives people for their sins and you're not able to forgive the people who took your brother's life. You're a hypocrite," Aunt Shirley lashed out.

"I'm surprised you know anything about Christ at all, Shirley," Abraham stated harshly.

"I know that He turned water to wine and I am forever greatly to Him for that. Cheers," Aunt Shirley lifted her flask before taking it to the head.

"Aunt Shirley is right, Dad, and you know it."

"I'm willing to forgive people for certain things, but I'll never forgive the bastards that took my brother's life, but I'm willing to forgive you for joining the FBI if you're willing to quit."

"I already told you, Dad. I'm not quitting my job and as far as I'm concerned, you need to quit being a pastor because you're not living what you're preaching."

"Wait a minute, Alyssa. I know that you're upset with daddy, but I will not stand here and let you disrespect him," Andrea jumped in.

"Excuse me?" Alyssa walked over to her.

"Don't tell Dad he needs to quit being a pastor. What he preaches about helps people in their everyday lives and lets them know that they can turn to Christ for all their needs, worries and concerns. No man is perfect, but daddy is damn near perfect and let's not forget everything he's done for us. You better watch your tone," Andrea stated confidently.

"You've got to be fucking kidding me, Andrea. Do you hear yourself right now? I understand that forgiving someone is not an easy thing to do, but if my pastor isn't taking his own advice when it comes to his personal life, why the hell should someone else follow his advice?"

"You knew that daddy was going to have a problem with you being a FBI agent. That's why you kept it from us for so long. We constantly tried to keep up with you and find out what you had going on. You should have been woman enough to tell us instead of keeping it a big secret. It's not just daddy that don't like cops, you see how many innocent blacks those bastards keep killing!"

"I can't believe you're really standing here defending him right now. For your information, I kept it from y'all because I knew y'all wouldn't support me, but I never thought it would be behind some shit that happened years ago. Unlike you Andrea, I'm not afraid to live my life. I'm a grown as woman and I will live my life the way I choose to. I'm not going to let our parents' run my life like they run yours."

"Andrea is living her life like she's supposed to. Our guidance is the reason that she doesn't have any children out of wedlock like most of these young people these days. Andrea is a very successful woman and unlike you, Alyssa, she wouldn't do nothing to deliberately hurt her father."

"I didn't do anything to you Dad, but you will be hurt by someone's careless actions sooner than later."

"Noooo you didn't just say that!" Aunt Shirley shrieked.

Andrea balled up her fists and stepped towards Alyssa, but Corey walked up and grabbed Alyssa by the arm and ushered her out of the living room. Alyssa looked up and saw that her mother, Alexis, and Anastasia was watching everything from the kitchen. Instead of continuing the conversation, she didn't put up a fight as Corey led her upstairs to her room where she began to pace the floor.

Alyssa tried to calm herself down, but she couldn't. The argument that she had with her father burned her up inside and she couldn't shake it for nothing. The lack of support she got from her father shouldn't have surprised her, but she figured he wouldn't support her because of how dangerous her job was or something on the lines of that, but it was for a reason she didn't think of. She also wasn't surprised by Andrea's will to defend their father, but instead of being the voice of reason, she just took his side and didn't try to defend her at all. What kind of lawyer was she? Alyssa knew it was only a matter of time before their relationship went back to the way it was. Andrea was always going to kiss their father's ass, but that was the final straw and Drea's uppity ass was going to pay. Alyssa began plotting her revenge in her head as she tuned Corey out.

Chapter 33

Andrea couldn't believe how the past few days had gone. It was true that they had some good moments, but the shocking truths had definitely outweighed the good. When she reached out to her sisters to come home for Thanksgiving, she had no idea whatsoever that it would turn out in the manner that it did. They had their differences growing up, with her and Lexi being the closest and Alyssa and Anastasia having each other's backs, but she had no idea that the middle sisters took the sibling rivalry to heart as much as they did. If she didn't know before, the Thanksgiving holidays had proved it. It may seem crazy, but she was already plotting thinking ahead to Christmas in hopes that everyone would come back on a more positive note. Maybe their dad's sermon in a few hours would make everyone forget about all of the drama.

Even though Drea still felt some type of way about how her parents treated them, she would never disrespect them. She didn't even cuss her dad out for the stunt that he pulled the Sunday before, so she wasn't going to let Alyssa disrespect him either. Andrea could tell by the slick comment Lyssa made during their argument that she knew about her pregnancy, but she wasn't about to be punked or blackmailed. They all knew how their parents felt about them setting examples. The pregnancy shit had Andrea feeling like a failure and she hadn't even had time to figure out how to break the news to her parents.

"We whooped that nigga asssss last night didn't we… couldn't even tell you was pregnant and shit the way you was throwing them blows," Lexi squealed.

"He deserved it… how you gon screw your wife's best friend," Drea shook her head.

"I can't wait to get that hoe… bitch better be glad she ran!"

"You know… we all have our disagreements, but we do know how to stick together when needed. I do hate all the tension between us, but I real life thought it was just a friendly sibling rivalry growing up," Drea expressed.

"It wassss… them two just special. Don't let them get to you sis," Lexi waved her off.

"You think everybody will come back for Christmas?"

"Helllll naw!!!!! You can forget that shit, Drea… I'm surprised the other two still even here!"

"Well Ima try… we getting older, mommy and daddy getting older, and we need to do better!"

"I come and visit anyway, but I'm just saying... it's gon take some good ass convincing to get the New York hoes to come!"

"Lexi be nice… it's Sunday."

"Sis, I'm just ready for Monday, so I can get outta here… all this shit has been a lot. I gotta get back to the A and find me somewhere else to stay. Bre bitch ass," Lexi mumbled.

"We all need to go out tonight… we all got shit going on, but we gotta be there for each other."

"Yeah yeah yeah… let's just finish getting ready for church. I prolly need to smoke me a blunt before we go just in case."

Andrea ignored that comment from her baby sister and finished getting ready for church. She couldn't lie and say that there weren't a million and one thoughts running through her mind, but she had to be the big sister and push through. Ever since they were kids, it was true that Drea took on the motherly role and tried to keep everyone together. Somewhere along the line, the middle two had started to resent her for it and it made her start wonder if she was really fit to be anyone's mom. After looking at herself in the mirror one last time, Andrea admired herself in her black dress she had picked up from Ross. She slipped on some Steve Madden wedges and sprayed some light blue perfume on and was good to go. Andrea walked to the kitchen and grabbed a banana and a bottle of water, then yelled for Lexi to hurry up.

They didn't even try to go to Sunday school, but at eleven o'clock sharp, Andrea pulled into the parking lot of New Jerusalem Baptist Church. Lexi was on her phone pretty much the entire trip. Drea knew that her sister was still feeling some type of way about her parents knowing the lifestyle that she was living, but she decided that she would talk to her at a later date about it.

"Come on, let's go," Drea prompted her baby sister, so that they could go on inside.

They walked inside and the usher greeted them with a smile and hugged them both. Andrea led the way up the aisle to take a seat near their mom where Anastasia and Alyssa already were. Devotion was starting and their father hadn't come from his study yet, which was good for them because they knew that he would have something slick to say since they weren't already in their seats. Even Andrea didn't get a pass on being late for church and she was the favorite. Andrea was very surprised to see Aunt Shirley at church. Lexi squeezed in and sat down beside her, so Drea took the seat on the end.

Andrea didn't miss the eye roll that Alyssa gave her when she sat down. She said a silent prayer that they would have a peaceful day and hopefully end the weekend on good terms. Abraham made his way to the pulpit right after the offering was taken up, wearing his black robe with red crosses on each side. He smiled at his congregation and took a stand behind the podium. Andrea recited his favorite scripture along with him, and when he was done, she knew that he was about to call the choir around to sing, but she was surprised when he took a different route.

"As you all can see, I have my entire family here with me today." He motioned towards everyone, then continued after there was a round of applause including some "Hallelujah's, Amen's, and God is good" cheers.

"My oldest daughter, Andrea who y'all see all the time, took it upon herself to gather up her sisters and get them home for the holidays. It has been an interesting few days, and I'm gonna have to pray for all of my children!"

"We gotta keep our children covered in prayer all the time, pastor!"

"That's right, Sis Buford!" he acknowledged.

"Oh shit… what is Abraham ass bout to do?" Aunt Shirley mumbled, but Drea heard her loud and clear and silently wondered the same thing.

"I want all of my daughters to come up here. I gotta do what the Lord has laid on my heart… Andrea has it altogether, but she's about to get married and we all can stand some prayer, right?"

"That's right pastor!" several saints said in unison.

"Y'all go on babies… he just wants to pray," their mom whispered to them.

"His ass needs prayer," Aunt Shirley said after she bent down and took a sip from her flask.

Since Andrea was on the end, she got up first, but she couldn't help but to notice that her sisters shared the same scowl that was on her face. She had talked to her daddy and told him that Joseph just wasn't the one for her, and he acted like he understood, but clearly, he hadn't. Flashbacks of the Sunday before ran through Andrea's mind as she slowly made her way towards the alter. She felt the stares of saints on her and her sisters and had begun to tune out whatever her dad was saying until she heard him say Joseph's name.

"Drea you stand to the left, and Lyssa, Lexi, and Stasia y'all stand to the right," Abraham said, then motioned for Joseph to stand next to Andrea. She took a deep breath because she felt herself getting ready to explode at any given moment.

"Why don't you tell him the real deal instead of going along with this foolishness?" Drea harshly whispered to Joseph.

Instead of him responding, she watched as his eyes locked with the choir director's and she shook her head. Andrea listened as her father went on and on and on about how she was about to make him proud by marrying the son of Deacon Jones, who was also his best friend.

"Daddy, I'm not marrying Joseph… he's in love with Julius!" Andrea blurted out before she could stop herself, while pointing at the choir director.

A series of gasps and ooh's and ahh's could be heard throughout the sanctuary. Joseph took off running out of the sanctuary while his dad stood there in shock along with Abraham.

"Drea… how could you? I would expect this from… why? How could…"

"From who dad? Me or Anastasia, huh… because we all know that Drea is your favorite and you got her sitting up on a pedestal while you look down on the rest of us!" Alyssa fumed.

"Alysa Holiday, you know that's not true… if you would have given me time I was going to…"

"I don't care to hear it… it's been this way for years," Alyssa kept talking while Anastasia tugged on her and tried to get her quiet, all to no avail. "Just so you know… your precious daughter that you praised for not getting pregnant out of wedlock is pregnant!!!" Alyssa continued and Anastasia finally put her hand over her mouth.

"You little…" Drea stormed towards Alyssa, but Lexi stepped in her path.

"Come on, Drea; let's go outside," Lexi whispered.

"Andrea… is this tr…" Abraham could be heard over the microphone saying, but before he finished the word, a loud thump was heard and he fell to the floor.

"Oh my God!" different people yelled.

"Daddy!" the girls took off running towards the pulpit.

"He's not breathing… call 911," was the last thing Andrea heard Deacon Jones yell before everything around her turned black.

To Be Continued…

Thug Holiday 2: Christmas Edition will be dropping on December 23rd! Be on the lookout… but until then, check out some of the work from the authors of this book!

Made in the USA
Middletown, DE
10 February 2022